A Country I

C000145910

Copyr

First Edition, June 2020

Copyright © 2020 by Anneke Boshoff

1

She turned up the radio as soon as she climbed in.

Said, I don't care where we go as long as we are flying.

She looked over at me like she'd never stop smiling.

Said, whatever you do, Babe, just don't stop driving tonight.

- Thomas Rhett.

A Country Romance

CHAPTER 1 - MASON / ELENA

My life is a disaster right now and I don't think it will get any better anytime soon. I am the CEO of Ashford Hotels & casinos. At 29, I am one of the youngest CEOs in the world...I am also the most successful. Also one of the most eligible bachelors, every woman wants me and every man hates me. I on the other hand don't care, I had a love, someone I would have done anything for, but that didn't go as I planned and I swore to myself that I would never fall in love again.

I used to be engaged to one of my rival's daughters, Zena Ledford, but I soon figured out that she didn't care about me at all. The only thing she wanted was my money and my company. I broke up with her after finding her in bed with none other than my cousin. I guess that is what you get when you get engaged as a business agreement. After that I didn't even look at a woman, not until I met Marley Jones.

She was the most beautiful girl I have ever seen in my life. Her long blonde hair and blue eyes quickly made their way into my heart and bed. We spent all our free time together, until I had to go on a business trip to London. My best friend Jake Forester, who is like a brother to me, stayed behind, he assured me that he would keep her safe. I was in London for two months and when I got back, I wanted to ask Marley to marry me. I had everything planned down to a tee. I got down on one knee in the most romantic spot in Chicago, but what she said shattered me into a million pieces. She couldn't marry me because she fell in love with my best friend Jake Forester.

So here we are heading to Montana for the wedding of Jake and Marley. Why am I still friends with them? Because I always put the happiness of my friends and family before mine. I am still Jake's best man and will smile even though I hate Marley at this moment. I guess in a way I dodged a bullet there and I can't really be angry at them for following their hearts. I just need to get used to seeing them together.

Jake's family owns a ranch in Montana and he has always wanted to get married here, hell even I thought I would get married here one day. But I don't see that happening anytime soon or ever. After Marley ripped my heart out, I have turned into a real jerk when it comes to women. I only needed them for one thing and that was to take care of my itch. They would scratch the itch and be gone. I normally didn't even remember their names.

My eyes landed on a beautiful property that was next to the gravel road we were on. It has a big cabin-like mansion with a fountain and pond in the front. From the road you could see the lush green fields around the house. The view is spectacular.

"Stop the car..." The driver stops when I give the order. I slowly get out of the car and walk closer to the fence. There's rows upon rows of trees, with a perfect view of the mountains right behind them. "I want this place." I state to no one in particular.

"I will get the information for you, sir" I turn to see my driver standing next to me. I nod, before I turn to get back into the car. The last thing I wanted was to be late for whatever Jake had planned.

We arrived at the Forester Ranch at last. It's still as amazing and beautiful as it always has been. I look around the open fields seeing a guy on a horse gathering some cattle. The mountain range is the perfect background to the green fields, the ranch has a stream running through it that has a big swimming hole a few miles from the house. I can remember all the summers Jake and I had spent in that swimming hole. We also lost Shadow there one winter. Shadow was the dog Jake and I rescued in junior year of high school. One winter he went chasing a rabbit, fell in the water and we only found him three days later. With the stream running through the ranch it makes it one of the most beautiful properties in the area. This has always been my favorite place to be, mostly because the sunsets and sunrises here are breathtaking. Not one is the same. Some Days the sky is painted in shades of pink, red and purple, other days it is painted in shades of orange, red and yellow with a splash of blue. I take a deep breath taking in the fresh air. It smells like freshly cut grass and pine trees with a mixture of rain. The stream offers the smell of rain all year round and makes you want to just lay outside as it relaxes you.

"Mason! You're finally here." I hear an annoying voice, I wish I would never hear again. I wish that she didn't become friends with Marley, but there was nothing I could do to stop them from becoming friends. Marley changed a lot after that and I guess she was just never meant to be with me.

"Zena, I didn't know you would be here already." I give her a tight lip smile. She walks over to me and kisses my cheek. She's a beautiful woman with wavy strawberry blond hair and pouty lips and green eyes. Even though we were together for about eight months, I never really felt a connection with her.

She links her arm with me as she pulls me towards the house. It's your typical Ranch style, two story house with a wrap around porch. The big windows make it easier to enjoy the view of the ranch. One part of the roof has been turned into a loft, where we used to spend hours just enjoying the view of the mountains or the warm fireplace. If this house could talk, Jake and I would be in jail right now. "Of course I would be here. Marley is my best friend and I am after all the maid of honor." She smiles at me and I feel like I am about to be sick. How did I last eight months with her?

"Mason, just on time." Jake walks out with his sister right behind him. He gives me a bro hug before I turn and give Sammy a hug as well.

"This place is still as beautiful as always. Where's Marley?"

"She's taking a nap. She wasn't feeling very well." Jake says as he walks off the porch heading towards the guy that was gathering the cattle. Something was bothering him, there was something with the way he just walked away.

I turn to look at Sammy. "What's going on?"

"Nothing, Jake's just worried about Marley. She ate something yesterday and has a little food poisoning. She doesn't want him to see her like that and it is killing him." I could only nod as I watched my best friend talking to the ranch hand.

I walked over to where he was. "Hey, you know that Marley will be just fine." He looks at me with a concerned look on his face.

"I know, it's just we are getting married next week and she doesn't want me to be near her at a time she needs me the most. How will that work when we are married? I want to be there for her in sickness and in health." He rubs his hand over his face in frustration. I can see his side and understand where he is coming from.

"Jake, she might just feel self conscious about how she looks. Maybe you should explain to her how you feel."

"Yeah, you might be right. I am going to talk to her right now. Take tonight to just relax and get some rest. The fun will start tomorrow." He runs towards the house passing the two ladies on the porch. Zena shouts something at him, but he clearly ignores her. I decide to head to the back door and up to my room. I was not interested in what those two wanted to talk about.

❣

The next morning I got up before sunrise. I love the sunrise on the ranch, ever since we were kids, Jake and I would get up early and watch our fathers out on horses just as the sun was peeking over the horizon.

After getting dressed for the day I head out to the porch. As soon as I step out the door the cool Montana air hits my face. I took a deep breath inhaling the fresh country air and taking in the silence, only the animals near the barn could be heard. "Guess everyone's still asleep." I think to myself. The night before coming back to me. My room is right next to Jake and Marley's room and let me tell you they were not quiet at all. I would say that Marley has recovered from whatever was wrong with her. I am happy for them that they both found love at my heart's expense, but why did my room have to be next to them. It doesn't hurt me to know that they are together, it's just that I would love to get some sleep and not be awake most of the night to them having a go at it. You would think being a week away from their wedding they would at least wait to actually go on their honeymoon before they start the honeymoon. Jake would always consider the fact that his parents might just hear him, But not now. Now he doesn't care that someone traveled hours to be here and might actually be tired and need some sleep.

"I need black coffee and lots of it." I mutter to myself, walking towards the stables to see the horses. The horses were one of my favorite things on the ranch. I guess that was due to the fact that I couldn't have one in Chicago. Every time we would come to the Forester Ranch, I would spend all my time either with the horses or on a horse. I kept muttering to myself how Jake and Marley kept me awake last night and how I needed strong black coffee as I made my way down to the stables.

"If you keep talking to yourself, people might just think you are crazy." I snapped my head up looking for the person to whom that sweet voice belonged, but there was no one around, just me and a horse.

"It wasn't you, was it?" I shake my head laughing to myself, while I look at the chestnut horse eating it's feed. "Perfect now I am talking to a horse." I turn around and head back to the house. I feel like I am going crazy. I just need to focus. Get this wedding over with and then go back home and do what I do best, work.

"Good Morning Mas!" I look up to see a smiling Jake sitting on the bench on the porch with a coffee in his hand. "You want to go for a ride?" Jake points to the horses.

"Morning... Don't know about good, but it's morning. But yes, a ride would be amazing. Let me just get some coffee then we can go." I head inside. When I get in the kitchen I grab a cup to get myself some coffee. I stand with my back towards the fridge and the back door. I pour my cup and bring it to my lips to take the first sip of this black gold, closing my eyes. I savour the taste, I have been longing for it all morning.

"While you're at it, please get me a cup as well... Thanks." My eyes shot open, that is the same voice. I turn around, seeing no one except the dog laying at the door. I shake my head again. I am sure I am going crazy. I walk out of the kitchen, I stop and give the dog one more uncertain look.

"I think this fresh air is not doing me any good." I sit next to Jake and take another sip of my coffee.

Jake looks at me confused. "What do you mean?" He sits back against the bench looking back out at the fields in front of them.

"I have been hearing a voice. It is the most angelic voice I have ever heard in my entire life. The type of voice that pulls on your heart string, the type you want to hear every single day. But every time I look there's no one except, at the stables there was a horse and just now in the kitchen there was a dog." I rub the back of my neck in nervousness not wanting to look at Jake.

"You sure it wasn't just someone helping with the wedding passing by?" I shake my head no. Jake chuckles as he puts his cup down before getting up." Well then Dr. Doolittle... Let's go for a ride." He claps me on the back before we walk off to the horses.

ELENA TATE

Ever since graduating college, my life has been one whirlwind rush after another. Not only am I the owner of one of the most beautiful ranches in Montana, I am also the only lawyer in town. I'm not in it to make money, I am here to help my fellow town people out of sticky situations. Mostly I have to deal with some land developer that wants to buy up some land and turn it into housing or even worse a mall.

I have only been back on the ranch for the past few months. I left right after high school, as I went to UCLA for college. My grandparents took care of the ranch while I was away. I had an idyllic life in L.A. After graduating I did my internship with one of L.A's most iconic law firms. For a while I thought the sunsets in L.A. were just as breathtaking as the ones in Montana, but now I know they aren't. I would spend hours on the beach just taking in the sea breeze and sun rays. A few months after I started my internship I met my perfect boyfriend. We had been together for two years, when his mom showed up with a perky blonde. His mom wanted us to show her around L.A. Well, my amazing boyfriend showed her around that's for sure, around our damn room most of the time. I am pretty sure she knows the ins and outs of my bed... and Ben. I walked in, took what I could and left him. I did however lose my friends, since we had mutual friends. I also lost an opportunity to work with one of the most successful CEOs in the world. I didn't know who he was, I would have met him the Wednesday after I packed up and moved back to Montana. Now I am back on the ranch and couldn't be happier. So here I am a 27 year old lawyer rancher and I wouldn't change a thing. Maybe just fall in love one day. I know the guy for me is out there somewhere.

I walk out onto the porch, the crisp morning air kissing my cheeks. It's still way too early for anyone to be awake, but I promised the Foresters that I would help around their ranch while they get ready for Jake's wedding. I can't believe someone actually wants to marry that big goof.

"Are you heading over to the Forester's?" Gramps hands me a cup of coffee.

"Yes" Smiling with appreciation, I accept the steaming cup of coffee, savoring the rich aroma. "I have to feed the horses and get something done for the wedding. I'm hoping to actually meet the girl who's willing to put up with Jake." I chuckle a bit as I take a sip of my coffee, before remembering the time. "I have to go if I want to get things done before anyone wakes up." Reluctantly, I set my cup down and headed towards my truck. It's huge, I basically have to jump in, to just get behind the wheel, but it works the best around here.

I drive over to the Forester Ranch, the sun is just about to come up. I park my truck and jump out, walking towards the horses to get them fed. I grab some hay and kibbles to give to Thunder, one of Jake's friend's horses. I hear a voice. "I need black coffee and lots of it." I tried to see who it was, but the hay bales were in my way. I didn't recognize the voice, all I know is that it's the most sensual voice I have ever heard.

"If you keep talking to yourself, people might think you're crazy." I call out before turning and heading back into the barn. I'm almost certain he didn't see me and when I hear him mumbling to the horse my suspicions are confirmed. I was definitely going to be able to have fun with this one!

I turn around in time to see him walk away. Dressed in a golf shirt and tight jeans, it was clear he wasn't from around here

After feeding the horses, I made my way to the chickens, where I found a man staring into the coop. For a moment I wondered if he was the guy from the barn but quickly dismissed the idea. The hair color and height were right but this guy was slimmer, built more like a runner than a man who frequented the gym.

"Morning." I smile. He doesn't respond. "Are you alright?" I duck around him and step into the coop

"Yeah... I'm alright." He runs his hand down his face.

"Are you sure?" He didn't look very sure.

" Yes... No..." He looks at me, a visible pain shining in his blue eyes. "How will I ever show them that I am good enough, if they won't even give me a chance?" Now I understand. He is Sammy's boyfriend; the city boy.

"Well, I can tell you one thing. Sammy cares a lot about you and one thing I know about her, she doesn't go for the approval of her family. She wants you and not what you can do on the ranch. That's what we are all here for. If you want I can give you a few tips around here." He beams at me like a child before Christmas morning. I fill the basket with eggs while explaining to him how to do it and we talk about what he does for a living. Turns out he works for Jake's friend Mason as his accountant or at least one of them. He met Sammy when she visited Jake a few months ago and they have been inseparable since then. He also finally introduced himself as Bazle Palmer. If that wasn't a city boy name, I don't know what was.

I finish with the chickens and say goodbye to Bazle. I walk into the kitchen seeing the stranger with his back towards me. "While you're at it, please get me a cup as well... Thanks" I ask walking through the kitchen to the dining room to put the eggs in the pantry. I feel myself hypnotized as I catch a whiff of his scent, it's a mixture between leather, fresh cut wood, and something sweet. I can't put my finger on the something sweet, but I have never smelled anything this captivating.

I put the eggs in the pantry as I have done so many times before, but today it felt a bit different. I know Jake and his friends have already arrived, and I have a suspicion that the tall handsome guy from this morning is one of his friends. I couldn't wait to meet them all, especially the girl that stole Jake's heart.

I went back to the kitchen only to see that the stranger had left and he didn't even get a cup out for me like I asked him. I go get myself a cup of coffee, thinking that he might not have heard me.

"Good Morning." I hear a faint voice behind me. I turn around to see a petite blonde looking right at me.

"Good Morning. Coffee?" I hold an extra cup in the air.

"Yes please. I'm Marley." She holds her hand out to me.

"Elena Tate. I'm from the ranch next door." I shake Marley's hand, before turning to fill her cup with coffee. "You're Jake's fiance, right?"

"Yes..." She looks around the kitchen not really looking at me. It was as if she was uncomfortable with me for some reason. "Do they just let you help yourself?"

"Umm... Well, Mrs Forester said I could make myself at home while I'm here to help." Her question caught me a little off guard. I rinse my cup out and dry it to put it back in the cupboard. I turn to look at Marley. "It was nice meeting you but I need to go.... Lots to get done..." I wave my arms around in the air to show that I will be doing something around the ranch, before I walk out of the back door. "Anything else." I mumble to myself.

I walk to the stables and see that two of the horses are not there. I take the horse Jake's father gave me when I was a little girl. "Hey Starlight, are we going for a little ride?" I lead her out of the stables and mount her. I just needed the fresh air and checking the fence would be the perfect opportunity to take Starlight for a little ride.

MASON ASHFORD

Jake and I came back from our ride. We dismount our horses and I grab a comb to brush down my horse. "We have people to do that." Jake says as he takes his horse inside.

"It will only take a few minutes. I like doing it." Truth is I didn't think I could handle everyone inside right now. I didn't want them to ask questions and I didn't want Zena anywhere near me.

"Hurry up. I am starving." Jake pats me on the shoulder. I finish up Thunder, before we head back to the house to get some breakfast. As we got closer to the house we could hear Marley's upset tone, not sure who she was talking to.

"I will let you handle that first." I smirk as I run up to my room to wash up for breakfast, Jake follows close behind me.

"I will deal with it once I am done with my shower." I laugh and close my door. On days like this I guess I am happy she broke my heart. I can't deal with how dramatic she has become the past few months.

I finish getting ready and head down to the dining room. As I walk in I hear Jake talk to Marley. He must have walked in seconds before.

"Marley... What's wrong?" He kisses the top of her head before sitting down next to her. I could see by the look on Mrs. Forester's face that Marley was not happy.

"There was this girl here this morning... I was trying to tell your mom that having her around here is a huge risk for all of our friends." She gives Jake a concerned look and I am trying to figure out what risk it would be to us.

"What do you mean it would be a huge risk for all of us?" I had to know. How could a girl working here be a risk to us?

Marley huffs as she stares at me. "Mason, most of you are wealthy. I can see a girl like her trying to seduce you just to get your money and the power that comes with your name." She says as if I am not aware of how women treat me. I shake my head as Jake looks towards his mom.

"Mom, who's the girl?" I could see that Jake was just trying to defuse the situation.

"Elena..." Before his mom could say something else, Jake's eyes lit up.

"El... Tate." He smiles back at Marley. "Baby, she's good. You don't have to worry about her. She's an old family friend." Marley arched her eyebrow at Jake. I almost laughed at the frustration on her face, but I contained it the best I could.

"Fine... Guess I will have to deal with random people being around." I choke on the bite of bacon I just took. When the hell did Marley turn into such a bitch?

❣

Later after everyone had their breakfast, we were all sitting around the table talking and laughing. Mrs. Forester told the others stories about me and Jake when we were younger.

"Y'all will need to pitch in and help to get the ranch ready for the wedding." Mrs. Forester smiles at me. She knows I might be some powerful CEO, but I have never been too scared to do anything around the ranch.

"Sure, whatever needs to be done, we will do it." Everyone groans at my excitement.

"Well then... I have y'alls jobs right here." Mrs. Forester looks a bit too happy when she looks at me and Jake. She holds out our assignment and I can't help but laugh.

We all head in our different directions, to start our given chores respectively. Jake and I walk towards the stable. We are the lucky winners of poop duty.

"Are you ready to shove or scope some poop, Mr. CEO?" Jake grins and hands me a pitchfork.

"You know a little poop never scared me." Jake laughs harder walking to the door of the stables. I turn when I hear the sound of hooves galloping into the stables. I see the most beautiful girl, dressed in jeans shorts and a pink tank top. I watch as she dismounts her horse. Her raven black hair blowing in the wind as her baby blue eyes lock on mine. That did it for me, I was lost in the gaze of a country girl. She breaks our gaze as she turns to get something out of her saddle bag, giving it to the horse to eat. "That's for being a good girl." She says as she nuzzles the horse. I swallow hard as my eyes wander over the silhouette of her body. The way the sun made her skin glow, made me feel warm inside. At this moment I felt as if I could get lost just being around this girl.

"If you stare long enough, she might talk to you." Jake laughs at me and I feel my neck and cheeks turn crimson. "Come on, I will introduce you."

"Elena..." Jake shouts. She turns around and smiles as she runs over to him. She jumps into his arms and I feel a tad bit of jealousy as he wraps his arms around her and spins around. Why am I feeling like this? I never felt that way Marley, she was always hanging on everyone.

"Jacob Forester. Just look at you." She squeals as she gives him one more hug. "It's been a while."

"Little Elena Tate. All grown up." He shakes his head as he looks at her. "How's your grandpa doing?"

"He's good. He should be over soon. He would love to see you and your fiancee. And I lost that nickname a long time ago. I go by Elena now." She smiles and looks past Jake locking eyes with me. I feel my heart racing as the baby blues pull me into her, I could drown in her eyes. There was something about her that made me feel like I wanted to jump off a cliff for her. Crazy right?

"El... This is Mason, my best friend from Chicago." He waves me over. I walk over to them and the closer I get, I swear she gets even more beautiful up close. Her hair has a bit of a purple shine to it, making her blue eyes stand out even more, she has rosy pink lips. She has curves in all the right parts, she would fit against me perfectly.

"Mason... It is so nice to meet you." I look at her shocked when realization hits me.

"It's you... I'm not crazy." I pull her into a hug. I feel her freeze at first but relaxes and hugs me back. Suddenly I realize what I have just done and pull away. I rub the back of my neck nervously. "Sorry..." It was all I could say. I just felt relieved that I wasn't going crazy.

CHAPTER 2 - MASON

She takes a step back from me trying to stifle her laugh. "It's fine. Sorry for not introducing myself when I spoke this morning. I couldn't help but laugh as you thought it was the horse talking to you. Anyway, I should get back to what I was doing." She motions around the stable, before turning on her heel towards the other direction.

I rub my hand on the back of my neck. "I still owe you a coffee." She stops and looks at me over her shoulder. Was I really asking her out? What the hell am I thinking?

She turns around to face me with a smile on her face. "I got my own coffee in the end, but thank you for the offer, pretty boy." She replies with a playful wink, then walks off again. Why did it hurt so much being rejected? She just blew me off and no one has ever done that. I shake my head and run after her. "Then perhaps some other time... Please." I give her my famous smirk that has helped me drop a million panties. She blushed and I loved the slight pink on her cheeks. She has an effect on me that no one else has ever had. I wanted to make her smile and I wanted to see her cheeks turn pinkish again.

"Fine..." She agrees and then walks over to Jake. I followed her to where he was standing by the entrance of the stables. "So, I met your fiancee this morning..." I could hear the sarcasm in her voice. I didn't even have to see her roll her eyes. "I don't think she likes me." I had to stop myself from snorting; it was true, for some unknown reason Marley didn't like her. Then again, Marley didn't like anyone who was prettier than her and Elena definitely fell into that category.

Jake laughs then slings his arm around her shoulders. "She will warm up to you." He was lying. Once Marley made up her mind that she didn't like someone that was it. She would make Elena's life miserable, and Zena would help her.

My phone ping and I read the message. *I have the info on that ranch you wanted. It will not be easy.* I shake my head. Of course it wouldn't be easy. That seemed to be the story of my life lately. Just once I would like to be interested in a property and have the sale go smoothly. I am not a bully, I would never force someone to sell, but I'm not above making them offers they can't refuse.

"I hope so... I mean she did manage to warm up to you after all and you are the grumpiest person I know." Elena's teasing of Jake brings me back to the conversation. Jake tries swatting her arm and she dodges him, causing him to fall in horse shit. They both burst out laughing.

"Elena, we need you in here." Sammy belts out from the front porch of the house.

"Well that's my cue… By the way, you two better start finishing with scooping up that shit. Wouldn't want to get on your mom's bad side." She winks at me. I actually feel my heart skipping a beat. I have to get my head in control and my heart needs to take the backseat. I can't catch feelings right now. I can't let what happened with Marley happen again. I will be leaving soon and then this will all be over.

After we were done with the cleaning of the stables, I headed inside to get cleaned up for the barbeque we were having tonight. Jake basically sprinted towards the house.

I walk in a few seconds after Jake. "Hey Baby." Jake leans down to kiss Marley's cheek. I nod at the other ladies in the living room as I pass by them. I didn't want to be anywhere near them right now. I know they are all supposed to be my friends, but in reality who would be there for me when I really need them. Only Jake… That's who. I walk towards the kitchen. I wanted a soda and then got cleaned up. I stop at the door as I hear music and someone singing.

I lean against the door frame, watching Elena Dance and sing along to some country song. I let my eyes roam over her body slowly as she swings her hips, bopping along to the music. I bite my bottom lip trying to get the thought of how I want to hold her hips against mine, letting her feel what she was doing to me, out of my head. She twirls, still not seeing me. She dances backwards and before I have a chance to move, she bumps into me sending us both to the floor.

"Shit... I'm sorry." She tries to get up. She's laying with her back against my chest and my arms are wrapped around her waist. I was not ready to let her go, I wanted to hold her against me for a bit longer. "Uh Um... You need to let go of me, I can't get up." She lightly taps my arms that's around her waist.

"Sorry... Let me help you." I move my hands to her hips. Putting one on each side of her hips, pushing her up. She stepped between my legs as I pushed her the whole way up, my hands resting on her ass. Can I just say she has the most perfect ass I have ever seen or touched. Elena turns and puts her hands on top of mine, giving me a devilish smirk.

"Are you comfortable there?" She asks and I pull my hands away, placing them next to me on the ground. As soon as I let go of her, I missed the feeling of her against me.

"Would you mind moving a little." I motioned for her to move a little forward. I was trying to get up without bumping into her again. Having her standing between my legs made things a bit difficult to get up. She moves away from me and all I want to do is pull her back towards me. I know that I can't and I have to stay as far away from her as I could, but she made things hard for me. "Are you hurt?" I tried to make sure there were no obvious bruises on her.

"Nope, but I think my ego might be a bit bruised." Her cheeks turn a shade of pink again and I love it. She's a natural beauty, not wearing too much makeup and she has a great personality too. She's sincere and cares about others. I might not know her, but I can see that she's a real firecracker. "Sorry for bumping into you, I didn't see you." She looks up and I can't take my eyes off her. Being this close to her, I notice that her eyes are crystal blue with small green specs in them. It is a stark contrast to her raven hair, which made her even more beautiful. If you think of Snow White, think at least a hundred times more beautiful.

"It's my fault, I saw you dancing and should have announced myself." I step closer to her, my lips hovering near her ear as I whisper. "I have to say I enjoyed the performance." I see her shiver and I can't help but smirk at the effect I have on her.

She shakes her head, dragging her finger down my chest as she bites her bottom lip. Is it wrong that I want to be biting that lip of hers. "I'm glad you enjoyed it. Maybe next time if you're lucky, I will give you a private performance." She teases as she walks away leaving me with a smile and a wink. I stare after her. How could a girl make me feel so many things without even trying.

"You have a little drool there." Jake points to my lip and I swat his hand away.

"Fuck you." Jake starts laughing. I want to get to know Elena, but I also know it will be a waste. I could just have fun for the time that I am at the ranch. She seems to be into it.

"Does the great Mason Ashford have a crush on Miss Tate?" I shake my head and run my hand through my hair. Did I have a crush? No, this was just an attraction and once I leave things will be back to normal.

"No... I don't even know her." I turn to look at Jake. "And you know me, I don't want the distraction of a girl. They are only good for one thing." I could see the irritation on Jake's face, but I don't give a fuck right now.

"Just remember... Elena isn't like the girls in Chicago. She still believes in fairy tales and true love. If you only plan on playing with her, just make sure she knows it and she's alright with it." Jake pats my back before he turns around to leave. He's right, Elena isn't like any of the women I normally hang around. She's enchanting, she captivates me in ways no other woman has been able to, not even Marley. I know I can't get involved with her, but what if she's it for me. What if she has always been the one I have been looking for? I shake my head to rid it of the thoughts of having anything more with Elena than a one night stand. I can't give my heart to someone again just to have them stomp on it. I know that as soon as she finds out who I am, she will change and be all over me. They always do.

ELENA TATE

I rushed out of the house after being that close to Mason. Dammit, does he have to be a Greek god? Everything about him is perfect, from the way his chestnut hair falls into his ocean blue eyes to the way his shirts pull tight over his toned chest. Here I go drooling over a guy that's going to leave in a few days. I am not the type of girl that has a fling, but for Mason, I might just cross that line.

Being that close to him just now felt right. It was as if we were made for each other. My body fit perfectly with him. I need to stop thinking about him, he could only be my downfall. I am a truly romantic person, believing that there is true love for everyone. I mean look at Jake, he met his true love even though he is Mr. Grumpy himself.

I look myself over in the floor length mirror in my room. "I look hot." I wink to myself. I am dressed in a short floral spaghetti strap dress that I paired with a pair of brown cowboy boots. My hair hangs loose around my shoulders.

I am heading to the barbeque Jake wanted to have to welcome everyone to the Forester Ranch. All of Jake's friends from Chicago are here, except for a few that will only be here for the wedding.

I park my truck next to a few expensive looking cars. I can't believe they made it on the road with some of these cars. These people are way out of my league. I made my way over to the bonfire where everyone was standing.

One of the ladies, I think her name is Zena, makes her way over to me. "Do you expect us to sit here?" She scoffs and points to the logs with blankets. Where else did she want to sit?

"Well... Yes, unless you want to sit on the grass." My voice is laced with sarcasm. I have been dealing with Zena the whole day, and had no time for her right now.

"I will do no such thing. Why don't you be a dear and get me something suitable to sit on. Not a piece of wood you are trying to pass off as a chair." She waves her hand like she is waving me away.

"Listen here, lady, I'm too good for you! I am not your servant. If you want something, get off your ass and go get it yourself." I state with a huff and walk away before she can say anything else. I needed some fresh air even though I was outside, the stuff people were making it, a bit unpleasant.

I walked over to the paddock that had some horses grazing. I wasn't standing there long before I heard someone behind me. I look over my shoulder seeing Mason walking up to me. I roll my eyes as he gets closer. These are his friends, even though he is sweet and handsome. He still hangs out with them, they are still his friends.

"What are you doing here?" I cock my head to the side with one hand on my hip.

"I wanted to make sure you were alright. You seemed upset..." His voice is calm and comforting. Why is he making me feel like this? He will only break my heart if I give in to his charms.

I shrug. "I'm fine... It's nothing I can't handle. I just needed to get away from the devil wears prada over there."

He lets out a sexy chuckle. Damn is everything with this man sexy. "Zena does love her prada... I wouldn't worry too much about her."

"I'm not." We stood there in silence for a few minutes. Both of us just stared at each other. My heart's racing out of my chest, this man is seriously the most handsome man I have ever seen. His lips are just inviting and I am sure a lot of girls have tasted those lips. I licked my lips involuntarily and I am sure he noticed it.

"I think we should head back to the party." I finally find my words and it's as if Mason has been snapped out of a daze.

"Right... We probably should before people worry. So anyway, shall we, My Lady?" He offers me his arm. A snort leaves me, but I finally accept his outstretched arm. We start making our way back to the party.

"Mason, why do we have to stay here? Can't we get a hotel or something?" That Zena girl pouts and reaches out, putting her hand on Mason's available arm. She pulls him away from me with a smug look on her face. She fondly strokes his arm. For some reason I had this pan of jealousy as I watched the two of them. I know I have no right to. I mean I only met the guy today and we haven't even talked that much. But deep down I do wish it was me that was on his arm right now.

"Zena, we are here for Jake and Marley. You're the maid of honor, how will it look when you aren't here?" Mason yanks his arm from hers and tries to push past her. She holds up her hand as she looks in my direction.

"Fine, I will play this little game. But when we get back home, we have some things to discuss" She stomps her foot like a fucking two year old.

"I am sure there are things that we need to discuss. It's a shame that you are not one of them." Mason walks past her straight to me, but before he gets to me Sammy pulls me aside. Which causes Mason to be stopped by Zena and two other women, I have yet to meet.

"Come on, Jake and Alex are about to make some s'mores. We can't miss that." I laugh at how excited Sammy was. I have to agree that Jake makes the best s'mores in probably the whole country.

I took a seat next to Alex. He was kinda cute. He has brownish surfer style hair that he has in a bun right now. The fire dances in his chocolate brown eyes that accompanies his wide smile. He comes across a little less stuffy than the other people that are here.

"El, you want one of my famous s'mores." Jake wiggles his eyebrows at me, while holding up a s'more.

"You know I never turn down a good s'more... Bring them here!" I beam up at Jake, taking the s'more from him. I slowly bite into it, careful not to burn my tongue. "Mmmm." I hum in satisfaction at the taste of the perfect s'more. I glanced over to where Mason was still cornered by Zena and the other two women. We sit around the fire in comfortable silence for a little bit, until I decide to broach the question that has been on my mind the whole day. "So, what's the deal between Mason and Zena?"

"Oh, Mason and Zena... Hrkk!" Alex jerks as Jake nudges him in the ribs, trying to do it without me noticing, but I am a lawyer and I notice everything.

"His father is close friends with Zena's father." Jake interrupts Alex before he could say anything. He cocks his eyebrow at me while grinning like a damn cat. "Why the sudden interest? Are you crushing on Mason already?"

"You're an ass, you know that?" I swat Jake's arm, chuckling a bit. "And to answer your question, I don't have a crush on Mason... I just think he is nice to look at. I am clearly not even his type." I try to give him a convincing smile, and it looks like he bought it.

"Right... Keep telling yourself that." Or not... Why did I open my big mouth?

"Keep telling yourself what?"

"Gah!" The three of us jolt up in unison and slowly turn around to look behind us. Mason stands there, watching us with curiosity in his eyes. "Sorry, for interrupting."

"Nah Mas... You know you are always welcome. Come on over and have a seat. I was about to make my second batch of s'mores."

Jake says as he motions for Mason to sit. How did I not notice him coming closer?

Mason chuckles. "How could I say no... They are the best s'mores in the world after all."

"I'm not one to brag, but you said it, not me." Jake proudly says. I snorted out a laugh. I am not going to give into Jake. He might make the best s'mores, but I am not going to give him the satisfaction of knowing it.

"You know mine is better than yours." I give him a challenging look. He smirks at me. Alex jumps up excited.

"I will be the judge, let me get someone to be the second judge. Maybe Marley would like to help!" Alex beams and quickly bounces away from his seat to probably go get Marley.

"I turn towards Mason who's still standing. "Well, don't just stand there, have a seat!" I gesture to the empty seat next to me. Mason nods and takes the seat.

While we wait for Alex to return, the three of us chat about anything and everything. Jake and I reminisce about when we were kids and how we would spend the summer out here on the ranch. We laughed at all the memories.

Mason was quiet most of the time just listening to our stories. I could tell there was something on his mind. He had received a text that looked like good news with that smile on his face. Every now and then I would catch him glancing at me. I tell them about school and moving back after graduation. That I am now the only lawyer in the area, while also helping her grandparents on their ranch.

"So, Elena being a lawyer and working on the ranch must take a toll on your personal life... Are you seeing anyone?" Jake asks, shifting his eyes between me and Mason.

"I have been on dates here and there, but nothing serious... Most men can't handle my career and my time spent on the ranch." I wasn't about to tell them about my ass of an ex boyfriend that broke my heart.

"But you are open to the idea of dating someone, right? Do you have a specific type?" Jake tries to give Mason a subtle wink. Why do I get the feeling Jake is trying to match me with Mason.

"Now Jake, if I didn't know any better. I would say you are fishing for information." I raise my eyebrow with a smirk. "You know you are getting married in a few days, right? I don't think Marley would be too thrilled."

"What? No... I didn't mean... It's not me. I'm asking for a friend." He stutters and I notice the look he gives Mason. I couldn't help the laugh that escaped me.

"Alright, since you asked. I'll let you in on a secret." I lean closer to Jake's ear and whispers audible enough for Mason to hear. "I have a thing for pretty boys with blue eyes."

Just then Alex returns with Penny and Marley. Penny is a sweet and friendly lady. Her long brown hair falls to just about her lower back and her hazel eyes hide a secret that she hopes no one will ever see.

"Ladies and Gentlemen, I present to you, you're judges." Alex beams as he waves his hand between the two ladies and himself. Jake smiles up at Marley as she walks over to him and takes a seat between him and Mason.

"Don't look so smug, just because I am getting married to you doesn't mean you get an automatic win." She winks and gives him a kiss on the cheek. She then turns to glare at me. "Although with the competition I bet your chances of winning are pretty high." She flips her hair over her shoulder which makes me internally roll my eyes.

"Great now that everyone is here! It's time to beat Jake Forester once and for all." I say and grab some crackers, marshmallows and chocolate for the s'mores.

Out of the corner of my eye I can see Marley watching Mason as he watches me move around the fire. I feel a tad bit of jealousy when she puts her hand on his arm. I have no right to be jealous. "How are you holding up?" She asks, making sure I can hear them.

"I'm doing good. The countryside is an amazing change of scenery." He smiles at me, even though he is talking to her.

I finished up with three s'mores but froze when I heard her next statement. "Mason, just be careful" I try to push it back. I try to believe that she wasn't talking about me. Hell, I don't even have anything to do with them. But the way she is glaring at me, tells me that she's warning him to be careful of me. I glance over at them to try and see his face, but he looks at her confused and she just smirks at me. "I can see your eyes wandering. I know you are hurting and the countryside might be good for you. I know, me choosing Jake over you wasn't easy for you. I know you are broken and I want you to be happy. But this will just be a rebound and you will never be happy with just a rebound."

I blink a few times picking up the s'mores I made. She just insulted me three times in one sentence without even feeling any remorse. What's worse is that she wasn't with Jake from the start. It sounds like she was Mason's girl first.

Mason gets up. He runs his hand down his face and yet again I can't help admiring the beautiful man. The way the light from the fire dances on his skin, it's almost as if it makes it glow and it makes the anger in his eyes look even more deadly.

"Not everything is about you Marley. Yes, I loved you and still care about you deeply, but you chose Jake and I made my peace with it."

She jumps up and gets right in his face. Everyone is just standing there watching the two of them. "Have you really? Because in my opinion, when you love someone, you don't get over them that easily!" Marley points her finger into his chest and I swear I see him vibrating with anger. I have no idea what happened between them, but she is pushing all the wrong buttons right now.

"Marley just…. Enough!" His voice is dripping with annoyance and his hands are balled up into fists. "Yes, you chose Jake and I respected your choice so now I'm asking you to respect mine. I don't need you to give me any advice on relationships." I look down at the S'mores in my hands and I know I need to do something. This is getting too heated and one of them might say something they will later regret.

"Uh Um…. Sorry to interrupt." I hold out the tray with s'mores. "These are yours," Marley grabs hers and takes a bite while she sneers at me.

"Thank you. I am sure they taste as good as they look." He takes it, causing our fingers to brush against each other sending an electrical volt straight through me and by the way his eyes just turned a shade darker lets me know that he also felt it. He takes a bite and lets out a soft yet very sensual moan. "Mmmmm..." He licks the melted chocolate from his lips. My eyes follow his tongue as it moves along the seams of his lips. Damn how I want to be the one to lick the chocolate from his lips. "This is probably the best s'mores I have ever tasted." I bite my lip as he takes another bite, this time getting some chocolate on his cheek.

"Um Mason, you have a little something... Never mind, let me just get that for you." I grab a napkin and stand on my tiptoes. I wiped his cheek with the napkin. There's a short pause when my finger brushes against his warm sun kissed skin. We gazed into each other's eyes, it's as if everything around us just disappeared. As if it was just the two of us here. I am sure he can hear my heart beat. He leans closer and I snap out of the trans I was in. I pull back my hand and turn around not wanting him to see me blush.

"Is everyone ready to vote?" Alex chirps trying to defuse the awkward situation.

Everyone stares at me and Mason. I swear I can see smoke coming out of Marley's ears.

I take my place on the other side of Alex, while we wait for everyone to give their votes.

"I vote for Elena! Yours were extra gooey." Penny beams at me. I like her, she's not like the others around here. I could actually see her with Alex.

"My vote is Jake. There is no one that could make better s'mores than my man." Marley blows Jake a kiss, before she gives me an evil smirk. Seriously, what the hell is her problem? I am not planning on stealing her man, he's like a damn brother to me.

"My vote goes to Elena. It was simply heavenly." Mason licks his lips and I know just from the look in his eyes that I am screwed. He is making me tingle all over and he hasn't even touched me yet.

"I have to agree with Mason. Elena's was the best. Sorry Jake." Jake fake pouts as he holds his heart. I do a little victory dance and Alex joins me.

"So, what did I win?" I suddenly stop and stare at Jake.

"Nothing... Why do you just want something? You are all the same, just want our money." Marley sneers as she walks up to me. I just have had enough from her.

"You don't even know me. Trust me sweetheart I don't need a fucking dime from you. You know what, I don't need a prize." With that I turn around and walk away from the group. Marley and her friends have been nothing but judgy since they got here. I don't need their money. I have enough of my own, but I don't go around shoving it in everyone's faces. She needs to wake up and smell the cow shit.

I made it halfway back to my truck when I heard someone call my name. I stop and turn to see Mason running towards me.

"Where are you going?" He asks as he makes it up to me.

"I'm heading home. It's been a long day." I start walking to my truck again. Mason follows me, but doesn't say a word.

"I'm sorry about Marley...." I stop and turn to look at Mason.

"You don't have to apologize. This is all her and she has a problem with me. Not that I know why. But you do not apologize for her." I stop when I get to my truck. He looks at me and runs his hand down his face.

"Are you sure you have to leave?" He gives me these hopeful puppy dog eyes. How am I supposed to say no to that?

"You want to go for a ride with me?" I open my door and wait for him to answer.

"Where are we going?" He walks to the passenger side and I jump into the driver's side.

"I want to show you one of my favorite places." I wait for him to close his door before I start the truck and drive off. The drive is spent in silence, but a comfortable silence.

I park the truck and motion for Mason to get out. We walk to the bed of the truck and he helps me lower the tailgate. I jumped up and took a seat. We are at the top of one of the pastures on the Forester Ranch. Mason jumps up next to me, he is so close that his leg brushes against mine every time he moves. We are parked right at the edge of a pond. The moonlight plays in the small waves of the water. The place always calms me down.

"So, this is your favorite spot?" He asks as he looks out at the view.

"It's one of my top five on this ranch." I watch as the firefly comes to life. Mason gasps next to me, grabbing my hand. I was shocked but didn't pull it away from him. Why? I have no idea.

"Where's the other four?" He plays with my fingers as both of us stare out on the water.

"It's a secret. If you stick around long enough to earn my trust, I might show them to you." I finally look at him and give him a flirtatious wink.

"Why is Marley acting the way she is with you?" I decided to ask the question that was on my mind.

"She's just a little overprotective of me." He says not even glancing at me. I could still see the sadness in his eyes as he stared out over the water.

"Just a little?" I raise my eyebrow at him. "Every time she looks at me, she looks like she wants to strangle me."

Mason chuckles. "I wouldn't worry about it... She will lose interest soon enough and move on."

"I hope so. What's the deal between the two of you? Did you guys used to date or something before this?"

"What... What would make you think so?" Mason sputters.

"I overheard the two of you talking. I guess everyone heard you talking. Plus, it's kind off hard to ignore the whole body language thing you two have going on." I reply and lift my hands in defence. "No judgment if you did and also you don't have to tell me if you don't want to."

I could see Mason hesitate for a bit. It seems as if this is hard for him and I can only imagine what he must be going through. "The truth is.... Yes... We did have something. She used to be my girlfriend..." His hold on my hand tightens. "I was so fucking in love with her. I was ready to give her anything she wanted. I had to go on a business trip. We spoke on the phone everyday and not one single day did I think something was wrong. I had decided that when I got back I was going to ask her to marry me. When I got back, she was happy to see me and things were normal. I took her out to dinner. After dinner I took her to our special place, I got down on one knee and poured my heart out to her." He takes a deep breath and I could feel the tension rolling off him. "After I asked her to marry me she told me she couldn't because she was in love with Jake. They had spent a lot of time together and she wanted to marry him..." I feel my heart break for him. But him being here for Jake and still treating them with respect says something about him. He is obviously a much better person than what they are.

"Do you still love her?" My voice cracks as I remember my own betrayal from the one I thought loved me.

"I do love her and she will always have a place in my heart. But I am not in love with her anymore. I guess I just love her as a friend or even as someone I know. It isn't romantic at all. In a way I am glad I dodged that bullet.

Especially when I see how much she has changed in the last few months." He glanced over at me with a slight smile on his face. He should really smile more, it lights up his face.

"Well, if you ask me. Jake and Marley are lucky to have someone like you as their friend. You're a good man. This might sound cheesy but if you ever fall in love again, whoever you fall in love with, that woman would be one lucky lady." I smile and give his hand a little squeeze.

"I don't plan on falling in love again." I feel like the wind is knocked out of me. Has he been hurt so badly that he feels like he will never find a love that would love him back. Guess I will just have to show him that true love is out there. Even if I am not his one true love and even if I get hurt in the process. He needs to feel love, real love.

CHAPTER 3 - MASON

I stare out over the water as the fireflies dance in the moonlight. I am still holding Elena's hand even though I have no idea why. I just told her my sob story about how Marley and Jake betrayed me. How I am still friends with Jake and want them both to be happy. She had to ruin it by telling me that when I fall in love again, that woman would be lucky to have me.

I won't ever fall in love again. I am not made to be loved or even to love someone. I don't know what Elena thinks will happen, but there is not going to be anything between us.

"I think we need to head back." I let go of her hand and jumped off the tailgate. I don't even wait for her. It would be best if she sees me as some kind of jerk. I hear her let out a sigh as she jumps off the tailgate and walks towards the driver's side.

"You know that people break up and find love all the time. You aren't the only one." She says as she starts the truck. What does she know? She's some ranch hand that plays lawyer.

"Yeah, well not everyone is me. Not everyone has the money I have. Women only want me for money or power." I state as I watch her roll her eyes while she's driving.

"Don't flatter yourself. Not everyone cares about that. You are too busy being self centered to realize there are good people out there. One day you will wake up and see you could have had something great, but your stubbornness cost you everything." She parks the truck and looks at me as if she's waiting for something.

"What would you know? You have the perfect life right here. Nothing to worry about." She chuckles and shakes her head, before she narrows her eyes at me.

"That's what you think... I had a love once... He cheated on me with some perky blonde his mom asked him to show around L.A. He ended up showing her all over our room and his fucking dick. So don't tell me I have a perfect life. I just chose to learn from my bad experience and move on." I swallow as she stares at me. I feel like an ass right now. I didn't even know that she went through something like that. She doesn't look like it affected her at all. "Now get the fuck out of my truck. I need to go home" She basically pushes me out and pulls the door shut as soon as I am out. I couldn't do anything but stare at her as she drove off. I have this feeling deep in my chest, one that I have never had before. Is this what rejection feels like? I didn't even feel like this the day Marley rejected my proposal. What is she doing to me? Why would I even care? I can have any girl out there, but for some reason I want Elena.

I watch as her tail lights disappear. "What did you do?" Jake puts his hand on my shoulder staring in the direction I am staring.

"I was a jerk. We were having a moment and I got scared. I can't have my heart broken again." I glance at him and he nods his head. I could see the guilt dancing in his eyes. "Don't do that. I forgave you and I am happy for you. You can't choose who you fall in love with. Do I think you should have told me before I proposed to her. Fuck yes. But what's done is done. We have moved on." Jake only nods and I know he still feels guilty. Shit, I still feel hurt and betrayed. But I am happy that he finally found the love of his life. I also guess I know deep down that Marley was never right for me. That she was never meant to be mine. I see that now. Now that the smallest things she does irritates me.

"Just a word of advice. Elena isn't like the women you are used to. She loves with her whole heart. Once you have her as a friend, you will have her forever. But if you betray her or hurt her. She will walk away and when she does.... She walks away forever. There is no going back after that." He pats my shoulder as he turns around and walks back towards the house.

Just as I am about to walk back to the house my phone starts ringing. I take it out and see Benjamin's name flashing on my phone. He is my lawyer who handles all my transactions.

"Benjamin... What do you have for me?" I answered the phone. I have asked him to make an appointment with the ranch next door. I want to make them an offer. But I want Benjamin to deal with them. They might be at the wedding. I haven't even tried to find out who's ranch it is.

"I have a meeting with the owner in the morning. I have just arrived." He sounds tired. Guess his new girl is keeping him on his toes.

"Wonderful. Make the offer and let me know. I am leaving you to do this, but if I need to I will step in." I hope I don't have to. I love the view and the location of the ranch. I could see it being a luxury hotel and spa. It's peaceful out there, just what you would need to relax.

"I will do what I have to, to make sure they take the offer." Why does that scare me? His tone was a bit sadistic.

"You know that I don't bully people into selling to me. If they refuse, I will step in to see if we can come to a compromise. I don't take anything by force." I state in an authoritative tone.

"Yes, sure. I will do this legally." He answers. Benjamin wasn't my first choice in lawyer, but the one I wanted left just before my meeting with the company and they assured me that Benjamin was just as good as the one I wanted. He has been with me for a few months now and hasn't let me down yet. But he also hasn't gone solo on anything.

"Alright, I will speak to you after the meeting. Have a good night." I ended the call not wanting to talk to him anymore. I am going to try and get some sleep. And maybe tomorrow I will get a chance to apologize to Elena for being a jerk today.

I walk into the house to find Zena and Marley in the living room. "Mason... Come sit next to me." Zena pats the seat next to her and I feel my insides turn to stone. I can't stand her and she doesn't seem to get the picture.

"No, I'm heading to bed." He walked a few more steps before she said the words I wanted to hear from Elena.

"Do you want me to keep you company tonight?" She runs her hand down the front of her shirt in a seductive way. I feel the bile rise. I have never been like this. I would have taken her up and fucked her just to get my release. But for some reason all I can think of is Elena. How I want Elena to be here with me. How I want her body pressed up against me. How I just want to hold her. What the fuck is wrong with me? I don't just hold women. Not since Marley ripped my heart out. I fuck and forget them.

"No, I am tired." I take a few more steps before I stop and turn back towards them. "I won't ever need your company again. You and I both know that you have nothing I want." I say with disgust. Zena will never have me again. She had me and used me.

"And Elena does?" She snarls at me. "She's a goody two shoes. She won't let you wet your dick and then forget about her. She's going to let you fuck her and then tell you she's pregnant just to get your money." The venom drips from her voice and it makes my blood boil. She knows nothing about Elena.

I take a few steps closer towards Zena. "You know what? That is something I know you would do. Elena is nothing like you. She respects herself too much to do that. You on the other hand would do that just to trap the man." She stares at me with wide eyes and I smirk. She knows I am telling her the truth.

"Now good night ladies." I turned around and headed up stairs before either of them could say something. I have no idea what has gotten into these women. They have all become territorial. Marley and Zena are the worst and Zena doesn't even have someone that is hers. I shudder just thinking of her touching me.

I walk into my room and laugh at the ear plugs on the bed. I grab the note that was with them. ***I thought you might need them. Sorry for being too loud. Jake*** I put them on the nightstand, before I strip. I get under the covers grabbing the ear plugs before I settle in bed. My mind goes to the raven haired beauty. They way her smile lights up a room. How her laugh gives me goosebumps. The way she bites her lip when she's nervous or thinking really hard. I can't get her out of my head. I swore to never fall in love again. Why am I thinking of a girl I haven't even kissed yet. Why do I feel like I need to be next to her, just to feel normal?

I finally drift off to sleep. My dreams are filled with Elena Tate.

ELENA TATE

I woke up the next morning to my alarm going off. I have a meeting with some lawyer that didn't want to leave his name, later today. He is already pissing me off and I haven't even met him. I have no idea what he wants, but my granddad raised me well. I will hear him out.

I get out of bed and head to the bathroom to get ready for the day. I could already smell the bacon grandpa is making downstairs. After getting dressed in some jeans and t-shirt, I grab my boots and cowboy hat to put them on. I head downstairs just as the doorbell goes off.

I open the door and see the last person I ever wanted to see. "Ben... What are you doing here?" His eyes go wide when he sees me, before he straightens himself. His demeanor turns cold as he fixes his tie.

"Miss Tate. I would like to see the owner of the ranch. I have a meeting with him." I try to keep myself from smiling. This just got a whole lot more interesting than what it was.

"Well Ben. Around here we call people by their names. I am Elena and you are Ben. As for the owner of the ranch. You are looking at her." I hold out my hand for him to shake but he just stares at me with this dumb look on his face. Why in the world did I ever fall for this man.

"Stop joking. We all know you are a lawyer and you don't own shit. Who is in charge around here?" He pushes my hand away and tries to push me out of the way. I block the door and square my shoulders. If he thinks he can treat me like shit or just walk over me because we have a history, then he has another thing coming.

I put my hand against his chest to stop him from entering. "You have an appointment with me. I am the owner of Monroe Ranch. Yes, it's mine. It was my mom's before she married my father. Since their deaths, this all belongs to me now. Is there anything else you want to know?" I say as I give him a daring look. One wrong word and I will kick his ass right out the gates of my ranch.

"Fine, I will play your game. I still don't believe you, but can we sit somewhere?"

"You two can take a seat on the porch. I will bring breakfast out to you." Grandpa walks out of the kitchen with two cups of coffee. I grab mine and before Ben can say anything grandpa gives him a look telling him to not even try.

I step out of the house and head to the table on the porch. I motion for Ben to sit down. He takes a seat and takes out a file. I don't know what to expect, but I know whatever he might have to say to me. My answer will be a big fat no.

"How have you been? I miss you…" I spit the sip of coffee I have just taken out as I stare at him.

"You miss me… Did you miss me when you were balls deep inside your friend? You lost the chance to know about my life the moment you decided to put your dick inside another woman." I take a deep breath and before he can say anything, I continue. "Now, tell me why you came all the way from L.A to see me."

He stares at me for a moment before he opens his file. "My client would like to make you an offer for the ranch…." I laugh out loud. I mean full on crying with laughter. "What's so funny?"

"You can tell your client that I am not interested. This ranch is not going anywhere. My kids will take over one day." Just then grandpa walks out with two plates of breakfast. He puts it down in front of me and

Ben. He gives me his best is everything alright look and I give him a slight nod.

"Elena, this is your best option. They are willing to pay a lot for this ranch. You would be stupid not to accept it." He pushes the document towards me. I take it and push it back towards him.

"You are welcome to have your breakfast. But after that you get the fuck off my property. I am not planning to go anywhere." I grab my toast as I know I need to be at the Forester ranch in an hour. Grandpa will show you out." I turn and leave. I'm seething right now. How dare he tell me what to do with my ranch.

I get into my truck and drive off towards the Forester ranch. I know I will have to deal with Zena, Marley and Mason today. On the bright side they are better than Ben. Just as I pull up I see Mason on the phone while he gets into a SUV with Alex. Guess I won't have to see him soon.

I'm not sure how I feel about it. I wanted to see him. For some reason I have a craving to spend as much time with him as I can. I know in the end I will be hurt, but for now it feels right just being near him.

CHAPTER 4 - MASON

I wake up with the first ray of sunbeams that filter through the window. I have always loved early mornings on the ranch. I might not have been here in a long time, but I still remember every day I did spend on this ranch.

I get out of bed and head to the bathroom. I needed to get ready, just in case Benjamin needed me. I hope he doesn't, that he can handle this on his own. I pay him enough to handle these types of deals on his own.

After a quick shower, I put on a pair of jeans and a blue flannel shirt. As I was about to put my boots on I heard a faint knock on my door.

"Mason..." I hear Zena's screeching voice on the other side. I roll my eyes, as I pull my boots on my feet. I get up from the chair and walk over to the door. I swing it open and wait for Zena to say something. "You're awake and dressed." She bats her eyelashes at me.

"What do you want?" I am in no mood to deal with her right now. She just doesn't get the picture. I don't want her at all.

"I wanted to know what your plans are for today." She runs her hand down the front of my shirt. I gently grab her wrist and remove her hand.

"I have business to deal with and then I am hoping to spend some time with Jake only."

"What about tonight? We can do something then." She gives me this hopeful look. Maybe I should just give in this once. I need a release and she is more than willing to give it to me.

"I..." Before I can answer her my phone starts ringing. I grab it and see Benjamin's name flashing on the screen. "How did it go?"

"Not good. They didn't even listen to me." He sounds frustrated. I run my hand down my face as I let out a disappointed sigh.

"Where are you?"

"Still at the ranch. I am having breakfast then I need to leave." I push Zena out of my room as I close my door and head towards the stairs.

"Mason?" She gives me a confused look.

I hold my hand over the speaker of the phone as I turn my attention to her. There is no way I am spending a night with that. "I have something to deal with." I turn back to the phone not even glancing at her again. "Benjamin, stay there. I'm on my way." I jog out of the living room motioning for Alex to come with me.

"Mason, maybe you should forget about this place. They aren't willing to even listen to me." I hold my phone to my ear when I see Elena's truck drive up the driveway. I glance her way for a moment, before I get into the SUV. Alex gets behind the wheel. "Mason.... Are you there?"

"Yes, listen, let me just talk to them. It's the perfect location. I won't even put them off the land. They can still work for me."

"I will wait for you. But the owner left. Only the grandpa is here." I smirk at his words. Even better, the old man will love the deal I have for them. There is no way he would say no.

"I will see you in a few minutes." I ended the call. I glance out the back window and see Elena get out of her truck. I need to talk to her. I don't know why, I just don't like the way we left things. I never cared what anyone thought of me, but I do care what she thinks. I will find her when I am done with Benjamin and hopefully she will want to talk to me.

Alex stops the SUV as we make it to the main road. "So, where are we going?" He raises his brow and stares at me.

"To the ranch next door. The Monroe Ranch." Alex's eyes light up at the mention of the ranch. "Do you know them?"

"No, but I saw that place and it's breathtaking. I heard some locals talking and the owners are well loved in the community. They have been around for years." Alex stops talking for a moment as he gets this faraway look in his eyes. As if he is thinking of something.

"What is it?"

"Elena is from the ranch next door. Do you think that she's from the Monroe ranch?" I never thought of that. I know she's Jake's neighbour, but it never crossed my mind that she might be from the ranch I want to take.

I sent a quick text to Jake. **What's Elena's surname?.** It doesn't take long before he answers me. **Tate. Why? Does someone have a crush? She's still pissed at you. What did you do?** I chuckle at his reply. I will make it up to her.

"Elena isn't from there. She must be from the other side." Alex lets out a relieved sigh. I don't know who between the two of us was more relieved, me or him. **I will make it up to her. And no, I don't do relationships or have crushes anymore. You should know that.** I sent a quick reply just as Alex turned into the driveway of the ranch. The closer we get to the house... No mansion of the ranch I can't help but admire the beauty of the place. There's lush green grass near the one side of the wrap-around porch. On the other side of the porch is a beautiful rose garden, with the most beautiful colored roses. The fountain I saw from the road, runs into a pond that runs past a crystal blue swimming pool. The pool is designed to give a beach feel, which is kind of ironic as the beach isn't even close to where the ranch is situated. I can see myself in the pool watching the sun set in the distance. The owner of the ranch does take great care of it and I can see the pride they have for the ranch.

"Mr. Ashford. You are just in time." Benjamin walks over to me. I raise my eyebrow as I see the nervousness in his eyes.

"What is going on? This isn't just about them saying no." He's sweating like a pig and looks like he might throw up.

"I might have run into my ex-girlfriend and she's still pissed at me." Of course this slimeball has pissed off some girl.

Just then an old man comes walking out of the front door with hate on his face. He reminds me of my grandfather on my mom's side.

"I told you to leave. Do you want me to escort you off the property?" The old man comes closer to Benjamin. He gives me a pleading look to do something.

"Sir, I am sorry. Benjamin works for me. Can you explain to me what he has done?" I take a step closer to the old man.

He narrows his eyes at me as he takes me in. "And you are?" He moves his gaze to Alex and a small smile appears on his face. "I know you are her for Jakey's wedding."

"Yes, sir." Alex answers with a smile.

I hold my hand for the old man to shake. "I'm Mason Ashford from Ashford hotels and Casinos." He takes my hand shaking it.

"It's nice to meet you son. I'm Mr. Monroe. But everyone calls me Gramps." He lets go of my hand and reaches out to shake Alex's hand. "Now I want this piece of shit off my land. I might just kill him for what he has done." I turn to look at Benjamin as he swallows hard trying to not show his fear, but anyone could smell it a mile away.

"Benjamin, what the hell did you do? I send you here for business not to upset anyone."

"I told you I ran into my ex. She's still upset about what I did." He half hides behind Alex.

"What did you do to the girl?" I pinch the bridge of my nose trying to calm myself.

He rubs his hands on his thigh as he looks at Gramps standing there waiting for him to answer. "I cheated on her. We were together for two years and then this new girl came around. I couldn't keep it in my pants and she caught me. The worst part is she didn't fight with me. She walked in while I was balls deep inside the other girl, told me to carry on and ignore her. She grabbed a bag and a few things she might need and that was it. The last time I saw her. She didn't even come to get her belongings. She had some guy come pack up her things and move them for her. I didn't even know where she moved to until this morning, when she opened the door for me." He hangs his head and I swear I hear Gramps growl next to me. Alex pushes away from him with disgust.

I shake my head. Yes, I might be a player, but I would never cheat on the woman I am with. I would treat her with respect and love the shit out of her. Just ask any of my previous girlfriends. "Was the other girl worth it?"

"No, not even a little bit, but now I am stuck with her. If only Elena would listen to me..."

"What did you just say?" I could feel my blood turn into damn ice cubes. Please no... Let this be a mistake. He didn't say what I thought he did. I just want to hear her name.

"I wish that Elena would listen to me…" Before he could say anything else, my fist connected with his jaw. Fuck, I did hear him right. He broke her heart. He is the jerk that betrayed her.

He rubs his hand over his jaw as he stares up at me. "What the fuck?" Gramps stands next to me and glares at him.

"You won't ever come near her again." I spit out. I clench my hands into tight fists. "And you're also fired. I will find my own damn lawyer. If you betrayed a girl you claimed to love. You can easily betray me." Gramps and Alex take a step closer to Benjamin.

"Get the fuck off this property or I make you leave." The three of us stare him down. I can't believe what just happened. I also can't believe that Elena is from this ranch and the girl he had.

"Fine. But you all will be sorry. I won't just let this go." Benjamin turns around and heads to his car. We watch as he drives off. My mind is reeling with how the hell I am going to do this. With Elena being a ranch hand here, I would have to make sure she still has a job. She could still do what she does now, she would just be working for me.

Gramps turns towards me with a questioning look. "Now, I don't know why that man was here. What I do know is, he was working for you. So why don't you tell me why you sent him here." Gramps walks past me. "Come take a seat and let's talk." Alex and I follow him as he walks over to the table on the porch.

"I would like to make you an offer for the ranch...." He holds up his hand and I can see something in his eyes. I am not sure what exactly.

"Let me stop you right there. I can't make that decision. This Ranch doesn't belong to me. I only help out here and take care of the place from time to time." He smiles at me. He has the warmest smile I have ever seen. He is the definition of what you want your grandpa to be like. "Tell me something... Do you know Elena?"

"Yes... Why does that matter?" I lean forward resting my elbows on my thighs.

"Do you feel something for her?" I freeze at his words. Why does he care? How am I going to tell him that I feel nothing for her. Hell, I don't even know her that well.

"Sorry, I only met her yesterday. I... She... We haven't really gotten to know each other." I could feel my face burn as I tried to explain myself. Why do I feel like a teenage boy being interrogated by my girl's father?

He just smiles at me and nods. "I understand. I have my answer. Now, get to know her better and by the time you leave to go back to the big city. You come talk to me again." The tone in his voice made it clear that there was no room for negotiations.

"I can do that. I will come see you after the wedding then." I shook his hand as I got up. Alex following me. "It was nice to meet you sir."

"I will see you guys soon." We walk towards the SUV with him following us.

I stop and look at Gramps, I look over my shoulder "Gramps, what is Elena to you?" I don't know why, but I had to ask him. He just smirks at me.

"Get to know her better and then we'll talk. Have a great day." He waves as he walks off towards the barn, whistling some country tune. I got into the SUV, where Alex was already waiting for me. He starts the car and pulls away heading back to Jake's family's ranch.

I couldn't stop wondering what Elena was to Gramps. Was she just a worker? Why does he care if I get to know her? All Gramps wants is for me to get to know Elena, that shouldn't be too hard. She's a nice girl and I had fun with her yesterday. I could get to know her and then after the wedding talk to Gramps. I will explain to him what my plans are and that he could still stay on the ranch. I will even keep Elena on as well. I have it all figured out.

A while later I am sitting on a hay bale watching Elena and Jake work with a beautiful snow white horse. Elena looks like a vision as she runs around the horse, her hair flying behind her and the dust that comes up to her knees. What caught my eye was the smile on her face. She's enjoying what she's doing. The horse doesn't seem to mind having the beauty try and put a saddle on him.

I haven't talked to her yet, not since I came back from the Monroe Ranch. She finally gets the saddle on the horse and Jake tells her to get out. She comes running over towards me and I swear I feel my heart skip several beats.

"Hey, you're back." She wipes her hands on her jeans as I jump off the hay bale. I stand in front of her and it's as if I am lost in her eyes. They are the brightest blue that I have even seen. I could drown in them and I wouldn't care. I reach up and brush a strand of hair out of her face, my hand lingering on her cheek.

"You're beautiful..." The words just flew out of my mouth, she gave me a small smile.

"Thank you." She says just above a whisper. "I should head back..." I don't know why, but I didn't want her to leave.

"Yeah... I should... I should probably head in..." She turns to leave. I grab her hand and pull her flush against my chest. She stares up at me with those intoxicating blue eyes of hers and I can feel the heat between us. "Could we go for a ride tomorrow morning?" I lean closer to her, my eyes still locked on hers. I move my hand to her hip, my thumb tracing smoothing circles on it.

"We can... There's a place nearby I think you might like." I smile as she says that and I lean even closer to her. Our lips a breath away from each other. She bites her lip and closes her eyes. There is nothing I want more than to pull her lip from between her teeth with my own. But I only lean closer and kiss her cheek, letting it linger a moment longer.

"See you in the morning." I straighten myself, before I walk away from her. *What the fuck Mason.... See you in the morning. Have you lost your mind? She definitely wanted me to kiss her and here I am talking to myself."* I mumble under my breath as I walk back to the house. I can't believe that I just did that. I can still feel her soft skin against my lips. I wonder what her lips will feel and taste like. Maybe I will find out tomorrow. I am spending the day or at least the morning with her.

CHAPTER 5 - ELENA

Today has been one of the most daring days I have had in a long time. First I had to deal with Ben, then I had to deal with Marley wanting a damn snow white horse to take her down the aisle. What does this look like to her, Vegas? Lucky for me, and I would say for Jake I was able to track down a white horse. Mr. Jensen had one, but it was still a bit skittish around people and a saddle. I have my work cut out for me, but I will have the horse for her.

I see Mason sit down on a hay bale and watch us work on Snowy... What an original name. After I get the saddle on her, Jake tells me to take a break. I run over to Mason and have a little chat with him.

Here I am standing dumbfounded watching him leave. "That's it?" He was so close. I was sure he was going to kiss me. Did I read that whole situation wrong? What is it about Mason that makes me want to be near him? It's like he has this pull and no matter how much I want to try to put brakes on these damn feelings, the more he pulls me in. I can still feel his soft warm lips on my cheek. The way his hand sends tingles all over my body. He was a walking magnet, and I just wanted to be pulled in by him.

I glance over to Jake and see him leading the horse back to the barn. I guess we are done for the day. I turn and head back towards my truck.

"Elena..." I freeze when I hear Alex call out. I wait for him to catch up to me. He falls into step next to me as we head to my truck. "Umm.. Could we go out sometime?" I glance over to him. He rubs the back of his neck nervously.

"That's a great idea." I give him a reassuring smile. "We could ask Jake. Marley and Mason to come with us." I tap my finger on my lips considering bringing Marley. "Though Marley might not want to come. She doesn't like me very much." He only gave me a nod.

"Sure... I will ask them. See you later." Alex turns around and walks away. I could swear I saw a tad bit of disappointment on his face before he left. I brush it off and get into my truck, driving off back home.

MASON ASHFORD

I can't believe that I just left her like that. I should have turned around, pulled her into me and given her the kiss she wanted. Damn, not only did she want that kiss, so did I. I want to taste those plum pink lips of hers.

I fall on the bed staring at the ceiling. I was hoping to get some sleep, that was until I heard Jake and Marley, only this time they weren't going at it like rabbits. They were actually fighting, what's worse is I could hear every single word.

"Why are you being like this?" Jake raised his voice slightly. I could hear that he is trying to keep calm.

"Because you are men and idiots. She's the new girl and you are all falling over her. Why? What hold does she have over you?" Marley shouts. I didn't have to pretend to know who she was talking about. I did know and now I have to hear what she has to say. I

76

know she doesn't like Elena for some reason, she made that clear from the get go.

"Are you serious right now? She's been my friend since I was a child. She's like a sister to me….."

"Really? Then why haven't I heard about her before now? Why doesn't Mason know her from the times he spent on the ranch with you?" I hear a punch against the wall. I am sure it was Jake, but anything is possible with Marley. "Why is she trying to get into any guy's pants that gives her attention? I have seen her with Mason, Alex and even with you. She wants any of you." Marley's voice gets even louder.

"Do you want everyone to know we are having a disagreement?" The edge in Jake's voice gives me the idea that he is no longer as calm as he was. "She didn't live here. She had her own life. We did grow up together. But she went to school in L.A and I went to Chicago. That doesn't mean she's not my friend. And you never asked about my life before you. As for getting into someone's pants. If you ask me, I honestly think she only wants to get into Mason's." The amusement in Jake's voice could be felt through the wall. I couldn't help but smile at hearing Jake say she wants me. "I am not saying that she's the type of girl that jumps into bed with anyone, but let's both be honest. She has only been flirting with Mason."

"How do you know what type of girl she is…. People change." I don't think Marley can really talk. Look how much she has changed in a few months. "Are you really okay with the fact that she wants to sleep with Mason? Don't you think he has been through enough? Mason is not thinking straight right now, he is still hurting and needs time to heal. She will just hurt him even more." I sit up trying to hear Jake's responses. Marley is going on as if I am a virgin and hasn't been screwing half of the women in Chicago. What does she think I do, lay in bed crying over her. She's quick to judge Elena, but she forgets that she's the one that broke me first. She's the one that ripped my heart out and made me swear off love forever… or at least for now.

"Marley, that is rich coming from you. Did you forget that we are the ones that hurt Mason. We are the ones that are rubbing our relationship in his face. And yet he still stands by us. He is still here for us. You know as well as I do, that Mason won't do something he doesn't want to do. He is not some fragile, insecure boy that needs his ex to stand up for him. From what I have seen, Mason likes Elena and it seems like she likes him as well. Let them be. He's an adult, he doesn't need you to be his mother." Jake says calmly, it was almost as if he was hurt. "I think you should give her a chance. You might be surprised." I could barely hear the last part with how soft he was talking. I hear the door slam, figuring that Jake probably walked out of the room.

"Jake get back here…. Don't you dare walk away from me." Yeah, that's going to make him come back. The door slams again, before everything goes quiet.

I fall back on the bed, trying to figure out what the hell just happened. Marley almost seems jealous of Elena. It was like she didn't want me to move on. Not that I am thinking of moving on, but there is something about Elena that pulls me in. She makes me want to be around her. She makes me forget that I don't want to fall in love. With Elena on my mind I drift off to sleep.

Over the next few days Elena and I spent every morning together. We would go for a ride just to watch the sunrise together. That became sort of our thing. She showed me a few of her favorite places around the ranch, telling me she is keeping the best for last. She also told me the story behind Jake's dad giving her Starlight. She went for a ride and fell off of starlight, breaking her leg. Starlight never wanted to leave her. The whole six weeks she had the cast on, Starlight would just be close to her, she would break out of her stable just to be with Elena. James, Jake's dad, decided to give Starlight to Elena; he knew how much she and Starlight loved each other. She kept Starlight on the Forester Ranch, due to the fact that they don't have stables on their ranch.

I walk out of the stables with Starlight and Moon Rocket. I smile as I see Elena walking towards me with a bigger smile on her face. These past few days with her have almost melted the rock hard ice around my heart. But I can't give in, no matter how much I like Elena.

"Someone's eager today."

"You said you were going to show me a special place today. Still not sure why I should have dressed like this." I wave my hand over my body. Elena arch her brow and bites her lip as her eyes roam over my body from top to bottom. My t-shirt hugs my chest and my swim trunks might be a bit too tight.

"You'll see... Now let's go. We don't have much time. I have a bachelorette party to get to. I also need some things for the wedding." She giggles as she mounts Starlight. I mounted Moon Rocket. I follow Elena as we ride over the open field coming to a tree line. She turns towards me, as if she was making sure I was still there. "Just be careful upfront.

We will go a bit and then walk the rest of the way as the horses can't go there."

"I don't think I have seen this part of the ranch before." I state. I hold the rains a bit tighter, following Elena into the wooded area.

Elena smirks at me, with pride in her eyes. "That's because you are now on the Monroe Ranch." She moves her horse along the narrow path. I smile as I take in the area. This will be a perfect addition to my hotels. This just makes me want the ranch more.

"Wow, this is beautiful." Elena beams at me, and now I can't even imagine her not being here on this ranch. If I do buy the ranch I will make sure that she stays. She will not go anywhere.

She stops and turns towards me. "This is where we get off." She smiles as I stop next to her. I dismount my horse first and hold my arms out to her to help her off. My hands linger on her hips as she slides down from her horse against my taut body. Her feet touch the ground, but I keep her flush against me. I smile down at her, my hands still on her hips. I could feel her breathing become faster and I am sure she could feel my heart beating against my chest.

"Are you ready?" I ask but not moving away from her. All I could do was hold her against me and drown in her blue crystals.

She takes one of my hands still on her hips pulling me with her. "Yes, follow me." We walked over to a cliff where we could see the lake. "What do you think?" She looks at me with admiration as I take in the area.

"It's perfect…. Are we going to swim?" I raise my brow as I see her walking towards a tree with a rope tied to it.

"Yes, we are going to swim. Now we take this rope and swing towards the water, then you let go. I am sure you can do it Mr. CEO." She gives me a flirty smile while biting her bottom lip. I feel the heat rise inside me. How I want to pull her in and ravish those lips of hers. I try to fight this urge I have for her. I am sure it's only sexual and I will lose interest as soon as I have my way with her.

"You know, I have done this before with Jake. We actually did it all the time, just not here." I pull my shirt over my head tossing it aside, before I take the rope from her. She picks up my shirt and walks towards a rock where she puts my shirt down. She turns and pulls her shirt over her head, before taking off her shorts to reveal her teal strappy bikini. If my pants weren't tight before they were ready to burst at the seams. I need to get in that cold water to make my extremely hard dick soften before she sees it. I tried to think of anything except her in that tiny bikini with her legs wrapped around my waist. I need to get a grip of myself, I'm ready to blow like a damn teenager.

"Uh Um... Are you going first or should I?" She inquired as she stood with her hands on her hip. Her eyes were roaming all over me and she was not shy about it. Her eyes widened a bit and I am sure she saw the tent in my swimming trunks.

"I'm going..." I make sure I have a firm grip on the rope. "I will see you down there." I need to cool down so I don't give her time to answer as I run and jump at the end of the cliff, swinging over the water. I let go at the right time just as I am over the water. I fly through the air before I hit the water, welcoming the cool refreshing feel of the water against my warm skin. I swim back to the top and see Elena at the edge of the cliff watching me. "Come on, the water is great." I wave her to come in.

She disappears for a moment before I see her come flying over the edge of the cliff. She lets go when she's over the water. I float not too far from where she makes contact with the water, watching her as she goes under. She comes up right next to me with the biggest smile on her face.

"That was fun. I can't think of the last time I did something like this." I smile warmly at Elena as she floats next to me. Our fingers brushing against each other, the cold water didn't help as I felt the heat radiating from her body.

"I thought you might like it." She said as she swam closer to me. I took her hand in mine as she got closer. Both of us treading water as we get lost in each other's eyes. I closed the space between us feeling as if she was just too far away, my leg brushing against hers as I tried to stay above water. I slowly brought my hand up to her cheek, brushing my fingers against it. Damn, she is the most beautiful person I have ever seen. I could feel myself falling and I am trying my best to stop it from happening. Rested my hand on the side of her face, and I leaned in. Only a breath away from her lips I searched her eyes for any indication that she didn't want this. Any indication that she wants me to stop. Instead, I was met with longing and desire, that was all I needed. Just as our lips were about to meet, we heard some ducks flapping near us.

"I think we should get out of the water." She gives me an uncertain look. Which is enough for me to pull her with me. We swim towards the shore.

"Are there crocodiles in the lake?" I ask while I help her out of the water.

"Nope, not crocodiles, but there might be sharks. We have never seen them, but they might be here. I have done this millions of times and never seen one. I just don't want to take a chance. Not with those ducks being that spooked." She smirks at me. I am sure she could see the horror on my face. She made me jump into a lake that might have man eating alligators in. "We are safe now. Let's head back before they send out a search party."

"Let's not do this again until we know if there are sharks." She laughs, shaking her head. She moves to climb up the cliff to get her clothes. "Elena..." She stops and turns to look at me. In an instant I'm in front of her.

"Yes?" Before she could say anything else I crashed my lips onto hers. I feel her freeze for a moment before she melts into me. I move my one hand to her waist, moving my other hand behind her neck to deepen the kiss. My tongue teases the seams of her lips asking for entrance and she willingly opens for me. Our tongues dance together as if they were made for each other. Her arms move around my neck as her fingers play with my hair. I pull her closer to me, wrapping my one arm around her waist. I move my lips from her jaw down to her neck. She moans as she arches her body into me.

"Mason..." I moved my hands to her thighs picking her up and she wrapped her legs around my waist as I pin her against a rock. I bring my lips back up to hers for a more urgent kiss. I could feel the heat from her core against my rock hard dick. I push into her even more, giving her that bit of friction against her most sensitive area.

Suddenly we heard the horses, I reluctantly broke the kiss, both of us trying to catch our breath. "I think it's time for us to go." She says with her eyes still closed. I give her a quick kiss before I set her down. We grab our clothes and put them on.

I can't help but wonder what would have happened if the horses didn't scare us. Would she have let me go all the way or would she have stopped me?

"You know we could always just stay here and forget about the others." She laughs and I feel my heart flutter just hearing her laugh. It has become my favorite sound. I need to stop my heart from overpowering my brain. I can't take another heartbreak.

"Sorry to disappoint you. I am pretty sure you will be missed. You are the best man." I grab her hand and lead her back to the horses.

"Fine, but I want to spend more time with you."I helped her onto her horse, resting my hand on her thigh.

She looks down at me with her spark in her blue eyes. "I would like that.... Very much." She leans forward giving me a lingering kiss that ended way too soon. She straightens herself and I walk over to my horse to get on him. We head back to the ranch and I don't know if I want to let her go. I don't want this day to end. I reach out for her hand, linking my fingers with hers as we ride back together.

We make it to the stables and see Jake heading our way. "Did you two have fun?" Jake wiggles his brows at us. I shake my head, smiling at him.

"Yes, we did. In fact, I made Mason swim in the lake." Elena laughs as Jake's eyes go wide.

"You mean the lake with sharks in?" Jake grabs me, turning me from one side to the other, clearly looking for something. "You seem to be in one piece." He lets out a relieved sigh.

"Really Jake! What do you take me for? I wasn't going to put him in danger. Do you not trust me?" Elena fakes being stabbed in the heart. Jake chuckles as she swats his arm.

"I was perfectly safe with Elena." I see the light pink tint on her cheeks, giving me a warm smile.

"Shoot, I have to brush down Starlight, and I have to get ready for the bachelorette party." She takes Starlight's rains leading her towards the stables. I stopped her before she could go in.

"Let me and Jake do it. You go get ready." I lean down, my lips against her ear as I whisper. "Go and enjoy a night out with the girls." She bites her lips as she leans into me. "I will see you in the morning." I kiss her cheek. I know it's a simple gesture. I just hoped she felt the passion behind it.

"Thank you both. I will see you in the morning." She turns and walks towards her truck. I couldn't take my eyes off her, remembering the way she looked in her bikini. The way she fit against me. How her lips moved in sync with mine.

"You got it bad. I don't think I have ever seen you looking at anyone like that." Jake puts his hand on my shoulder. Both of us watched Elena get into her truck. I didn't have it bad, I just have this desire for her. Once we get rid of the sexual tension between us, we will be over this.

"No, I don't. She's a beautiful woman and I like her company." That's all it is. I am sure of it. I can't have my heart involved here. It needs to take the backseat.

"Keep telling yourself that. For what it's worth, you won't regret it if you give her a chance. She's an amazing woman. I am pretty sure she trusts you more than anything and she might be falling a little bit. She took you to her favorite place. She has never taken anyone there. Not even I have been there. I just know about it, because her mom once told me. It was her and her mom's place." Why didn't she tell me? We were there the whole day and she never said anything. Can I allow her to fall for me knowing I am not going to return those feelings? I have to be very careful. I need her to know that if we do more than just kissing, it will only be a one time thing. I don't want a relationship.

CHAPTER 6 - ELENA

I had the most amazing day with Mason. I might be falling for him, as crazy as it sounds. I know we have only known each other for a little while, but there is something about him. The way he treats me. I have gotten to know him these past few days we have spent together. And that kiss... It was as if fireworks went off inside of me. It was magical and I wanted more, but first I have to get ready for the bachelorette party from hell.

I stand in my room in front of the floor length mirror making sure my outfit is perfect. I don't know how I will survive the night. I am just happy they chose a country bar to go to. At least I will know some of the people there.

I ran down the stairs seeing Gramps shake his head at me. "What's the hurry, sweetheart?" He holds a cup of coffee out to me. I take a sip from the cup and hand it back to him.

"It's Marley's bachelorette party tonight. I might stay over at the Forester Ranch tonight. Don't want to drive back too late." I give him a kiss on the cheek. I mean lets be honest, I don't even think i will stay at the party that long. "See you tomorrow. Are we still hosting the wedding party for lunch tomorrow?"

"Yes, we are. Enjoy your night and be safe." I wave at him as I run out the door. I was already late and I could already hear them complaining.

♥

I walk into the bar and see the ladies sitting at one of the tables, walking over to them. I smile when I see Sammy. "Hey... Sorry I'm late."

"Leave it to the..." Zena looks me up and down with a smirk. "Ranch hand to hold up a function." I narrow at Zena as she shakes her head chuckling.

"At least I showed up. I could have decided to stay home and work on the ranch." Before she could say anything else I turned and headed towards the bar. I needed a drink and a strong one if I plan to make it through this.

I decided to get drinks for everyone. Maybe I will be able to win them over or at least be tolerated by them. I look over to where they are sitting and see them all laughing and talking. Way to make someone feel unwelcome.

"Hey pretty lady..." I smile as I see John standing behind the bar. "What can I get for you?"

"Hey you... I already gave my order." I glance back at the ladies again and John seems to notice it.

"Don't let some city bitches put you down. You are amazing and if they don't see it they don't deserve to be in your life." I chuckle and give John a hug over the bar.

"Thanks John. I forgot how well you know me. Let me go back to the lion's den." John just chuckles and gives me a kiss on my cheek, before turning back to the other people at the bar.

As I approach the table where the ladies were sitting, I freeze when I hear what Zena says to Marley.

"Once we get home, I am sure that I will find a way for Mason to propose to me again. He has been hinting that he has made a mistake with breaking off the engagement." Marley nods her head and I feel my heart pounding in my chest. Zena was engaged to Mason, why didn't he tell me that. He told me about Marley, but never mentioned Zena. Unless he didn't care about her, or they weren't engaged.

I walk closer and put the drink on the table. Not one of them thanked me. I guess that's not in their vocabulary. We or rather they spend the night talking and drinking. I was bored out of my mind.

"If we are done here. We have some games set up back at the house." Sammy states and I see the others roll their eyes.

"Games are for kids. Marley wants fun, not to be bored at home." Zena smirks at me with this evil look in her eyes. I am sure deep down she's not as bad as she wants us to think.

I sit next to Sammy when I feel my phone vibrate. I take it out to see a message from Mason. **Hope you're having fun. I would like to see you after the party, if you're not too tired.** I smile feeling thankful that none of these girls want to play games. Maybe I can show Mason my favorite place to go stargazing.

Sure, none of these ladies wants to have an after party. Meet me on the porch in 20 minutes. I sent him my reply.

"Why are you smiling like someone who just won the lottery?" Sammy nudges me with her shoulder. She giggles when I show her the text from Mason.

"I think I'm heading out. I will see you all at the Monroe Ranch for lunch tomorrow." I get up saying my goodbyes. I see Marley narrow her eyes at me.

"Do you mind giving us a lift? I don't feel like partying anymore. I want to see Jake." I snap my head over to Marley. She is doing this on purpose and I can't tell her she can't come with me. That would look suspicious.

"Sure... I can drop you off." Marley and Penny jump up saying their goodbyes to the other girls. I couldn't help but notice the look Zena and Marley shared. Marley was up to something and I don't know what it is. We all head out to my truck and head back to the ranch.

MASON ASHFORD

I sit at the fire with Alex and Jake, waiting for Bazle to come join us. I stare at the flames dancing in front of me. All I could think about is the kiss Elena and I shared, no kiss has ever felt like that. Everything Elena does is consuming my mind. She's all I can think about. There is nothing I want more than to see her smile, hear her laughing and taste those perfectly kissable lips of hers. For some reason I wanted to be the one to make her smile, the one to comfort her when she's sad and the one that protects her and keeps her safe. My heart says fall and fall hard, but my brain says stop this shit, she's a woman and she will only hurt you like they all do. Have your fun with her and be done. Who do I listen to?

"Earth to Mason..." Jake nudges my shoulder with his, bringing me back to the present.

"Um... Sorry... I was lost in my own mind..." I stop talking and rather take a sip of my beer.

"Thinking about a certain raven haired beauty?" Jake teases. I shake my head. Jake knows me better than anyone and I know I can't hide it from him.

"Guys, I need to ask you something." Alex plops down in front of me and Jake. We give him a nod to tell him to go on. "So... I asked Elena to go out with me a few days ago..." I swear my eyes almost popped out from what I was hearing. Could I be jealous? No, I don't want more than a fling with her.

"What did she say?" Jake asks before I could even really process the possibilities. What if she said yes?

Alex rubs the back of his neck nervously. "Well, that's what I want to find out. She said it was a great idea and that we should find out if you guys would like to come along"

"Me and Marley, as in... a double date?" Jake's forehead looked like a map with the way he was frowning right now.

"Nope... You, Marley and Mason." I almost jumped up in excitement. Almost. I had to keep my cool for now. "Do you think that means that she's not into me?" The hurt in Alex's eyes nearly broke me. Alex is not like us or should I say like me. He doesn't just have a girl for one night and then forget about her. He wants true love. He still believes that there is someone out there for each of us. Maybe Elena would be better off with him, but the selfish me wants her for myself.

"Alex... I'm sure that it's not that she doesn't like you. She just might be into someone else." Jake pats Alex's shoulder with sincerity.

"That explains it. I just thought she didn't want to be alone with me." Alex lets out a wary sigh. I turn back to the fire. I need to tell Elena that there can't be anything more than a fling between us. I can't give her what she wants. Soon, I will be going back to Chicago and she will be here. Even if I do buy the ranch, I will only be here while the development takes place, then it will be back to Chicago for me.

After a while I was standing in the kitchen with Jake. We have the house to ourselves as everyone has something to do. After talking to Elena, I knew she would be back in about twenty minutes.

"I can't believe you spilled that sauce." Jake chuckles as he takes his pants off, standing only in his boxer briefs. I already had mine taken off, the damn sauce was still hot and burned like hell.

"Sorry, I wasn't paying attention to what I was doing." I wasn't. I was lost thinking about the crystal blue eyes that I can't seem to get out of my mind. No matter how much I try to do it. I wasn't paying attention to how close the pot was to the edge of the counter. Jake stood next to me and we flipped the pot spilling the sauce over our shirts and pants.

"I wonder where you were just now." Jake glances over his shoulder at me and I give him this goofy smile. "You know what... I don't want to know." I chuckle and grab a cloth to wipe the counter and the floor with.

"I'm going to spend some time with Elena after the party. I just want to spend some time with her."

"That's amazing, man..." Jake interrupted me before I could say anything else. He pulls me into a bro hug. He is reading too much into this, but I am not going to correct him, not now anyway.

"Um mm... Are we interrupting something?" Jake and I broke our hug just to see Marley and Penny standing by the door. Penny bites her lip as her eyes roam over my body. Fuck I forgot I am only in boxer briefs.

I try to find something to hold in front of me when I hear her sweet voice. "Marley, you..." Elena stops talking as she locks eyes with me. I give her a pleading look motioning with my eyes at Penny. She winks at me as she grabs an apron and throws it at me.

"Did you need something? Or are you going to stare at Mason like some perv?" Marley snaps her fingers in front of Elena's face and all I want to do is take Elena out of here.

"I'm sorry... I am the perv... And yet, there you are staring at another man when yours is standing like a foot away from him." She growls as she pushes a bag in Marley's hands. "You forgot your bag in my truck." Marley didn't say anything back. She just grabbed her bag and walked out shouting for Jake to come.

"Here we go again." Jake mutters as he walks past me. Elena, Penny and I stand in the kitchen, the awkwardness could be felt in the air. I wanted to go to my room to get dressed, but Penny blocked the doorway.

I walk closer to Elena trying to get her to cover most of my body that the apron wasn't covering. It was clear that Penny wasn't planning on moving anytime soon. "Please get me out of here." I whisper to Elena, causing her to snort. Poor Penny was probably shocked seeing a half naked man. She always seemed so innocent.

"Penny, will you excuse us please. I promised Mason I would show him where the wedding will be." Elena lies as she pushes me past Penny. I ran up the stairs as soon as I was past Penny.

"I will be right back." I shout back at Elena, just before I close my door. I grab some clothes and get dressed. I couldn't wait to get out of here with Elena. As I make it to the bottom of the stairs I hear Penny and I freeze.

"I would love to see where the wedding will be as well. You don't mind me tagging along." She asks in an innocent voice. Fuck no. I don't want anyone to come with us. I want to be alone with Elena.

"Sure... You are welcome to come with us." Elena gave her a tight smile. I hoped with everything in me that we don't have to take Penny with us. I take the last few steps, walking to stand next to Elena.

Penny turns and smiles at me. "I hope it will be alright for me to join you. I just want to see where the wedding will be held." She moves closer to me and bats her eyelashes.

I wink at Elena. "It's no problem. Before we go, Bazle asked that you help him with something for Sammy." Penny claps her hands together excited. I knew helping someone who's in love would get her excited.

"We will wait for you." Elena makes a move to sit down. She caught on to what I was planning.

"I should go see what he wants." Penny rests her hand on my arm. "I will be back in a few minutes." I nod. She walks up the stairs and as soon as she's out of earshot, I turn to Elena.

"We have to hurry. No one is here and once she gets to Bazle's room, she will know we tried to ditch her." I grab Elena's hand pulling her out the door with me. We were both giggling like a bunch of teenagers who just escaped the cops.

We jump in Elena's truck and drive off towards an open field on the border between the Forester Ranch and the Monroe Ranch. We drove towards a gate, I got out once Elena stopped to open the gate for her to drive through.

"The next place is also one of my secret spots. I have to admit, I have spent a few nights here before. Just wanting to escape everything." Elena turns to me as she motions for me to get out, before she gets out herself. I look up and I have never seen the stars this close or even this many. Not even when I was here before.

"This is amazing. It's unreal...." I glance back at Elena and see her watching me with a sparkle in her eyes. "What?"

She giggles and damn it is doing something to me. "I love seeing your reactions. It just makes me appreciate everything again, when I get to experience it for the first time again." I pull her closer to me, my eyes locking on hers. It would be so easy to let go, but something deep inside me is telling me not to fall, not to let go.

"Thank you... You have shown me so much in the last few days. Things I never thought I would see on my own." I wrap my arms tighter around her waist. Her tiny hands press against my chest, over my heart. And right at this moment it feels as if she has my heart in her hand. "Elena... I... You are something else." I see her cheeks turn a beautiful shade of pink. I have never loved pink this much, not until I've seen her cheeks turn pink.

"I do hope that I will still see you after the wedding." She looks up at me with hope in her eyes and just for tonight I want her to have that hope.

"I am sure you would." I mean it wasn't a lie. I still want to buy the ranch. My lips capture hers in a passionate kiss. Her arms wrap around my neck as I tighten mine around her waist even more. I break the kiss first, brushing the back of my hand over her cheek. "You are so beautiful..." Elena squeals as I pick her up, holding her close to me still. I set her down on the ground again and she gave me this mischievous smile.

"Let me show you the best way to watch the stars." She walks over to her tailgate and opens it. Then she walks back to the driver's side, taking out some blankets and pillows. She makes a bed in the bed of the truck. When she was done she motioned for me to come lay down next to where she was sitting. "Now look up." She lays down next to me. Our hands brushed against each other as we tried to get comfortable.

"I can see why you love this." I turn to face her as she looks up at the stars. Her smile lights up the night sky. It even outshines the million, no billions of stars in the sky. If only I wasn't this broken. I turn back to look up at the stars again.

We lay there looking at the stars and making small talk for a while. I learned that she has a gay best friend, who has been her rock through everything. Elena keeps moving closer and closer to me, all the while looking at the night sky. We play silently with each other's fingers. I could feel the heat radiating off her as she moved closer. Her closeness

made my head spin, I'm about to lose all self
control and take her on the back of this truck.
All I want to do is hear her scream my name
as I devour her body. I swallow audibly,
casting a subtle glance at her, my heart
pounding in my head and dick. I could feel how
she moved even closer, her leg brushing
against mine. I swear I hear her gasp when I
run my fingers along her arm. Our eyes stayed
fixed on the night sky with the billion stars
creating the perfect atmosphere. We were
dangerously close to each other, the heavy
silence hanging between us, the air electrifying
and crackling with barely contained desire.

Our hesitant touches became more
frequent to be considered as an accident. It
was making it harder to concentrate on the
stars. We rolled to face each other at the same
time. Her eyes were darker and full of desire.
Still a bit hesitant I cup her cheek, again my
eyes were looking for permission and I got it.
We slowly moved to each other, our lips frozen
just a breath away before our lips collided
together. The fire filled me as our kiss grew
more passionate. I was pouring all my desire
into this kiss. My hand runs along her back
settling on her ass as I pull her tight against
me letting her feel what she is doing to me. My
other hand tangled in her hair to deepen the
kiss.

I groan against her lips, feeling how her body grinds against mine as she melts into my touch. I gently roll her onto her back and settle between her legs. My hands run up her sides as I move her shirt to the top. We break the kiss only to remove our shirts. I lean back down, capturing her lips again. I unclasp her bra, taking it off in one swift motion. I move my lips against hers in perfect sync. My hands reach the waistband of her jeans and I expertly pop the button, she lifts her hips allowing me to slide them down her beautiful smooth long legs. I toss them to the side, all without breaking our kiss. My fingers hooked onto the sides of her panties before ripping them off with a sharp tug. She gasps with surprise, I catch her moans with my kiss. Without breaking the kiss I ran my hand up her legs, caressing her inner thighs and sliding them higher until I could feel the wetness pooling between her legs. I drag my finger slowly between her lower lips, my tongue thrusting inside her mouth. My kiss was pure burning desire, I'm not able to hold it back any longer.

"MMMM Mason…." She moans as my finger finds her clit and I lightly make circles on it.

"Damn… Already wet for me…" I put a bit of pressure on her clit. Without warning I thrust two fingers inside her. "Fuck… so tight…"

I move them in and out while teasing her clit with my thumb. Her body writhe beneath mine as she tries to get more friction.

"Mason... I'm... going to..." I feel her walls tighten around my fingers and with the way her breathing picks up, I know she's close.

"Cum for me, beautiful..." That was all she needed. She releases all over my fingers screaming my name. I am sure everyone within a hundred miles might have heard her. Her body shakes against mine as I help her come down from her high. I take her lips in a hungry kiss as she quietly whimpers in my arms.

Elena reached for my belt, unbuckling it before pushing my jeans and boxers down my legs. She gasps and I see the faint pink tint on her cheeks as she stares at my cock. I am blessed down there even if I have to say so myself. "It's not going to fit..." She says with wide eyes.

"I will be gentle. Trust me it will fit." I kiss her again, trying to help her relax. I settle between her legs again, lining myself up to her entrance. "Relax, beautiful... I will go slow." She nods as I press the tip of my cock into her wetness. "Shit, you're tight..." Damn, she might just make me blow my load before I am even inside her. I push in a little bit more and she moans

"Mason…. Just like that…" I could listen to her moan my name forever. I push the rest of the way in, I don't move as I give her a chance to adjust. She moves her hips letting me know that I can move. I start moving in and out of her at a slow pace. Our moans and gasps become louder and louder with each thrust. She's perfect, it was as if she was made for me. If only I could give her more. I pick up the pace thrusting into her harder and faster.

I hover over her body, my eyes never leaving hers. She wraps her legs around my waist as I lift her hips slightly to get a new angle to be able to hit deeper inside her. Our lips crash onto each other again as I pound into her not stopping my movements even for a second. I groan as I feel her inner muscles squeeze me tightly bringing me closer to release.

"I… I can't hold it… Cum with me…." I groan, breaking the kiss for a split second as I kneel between her legs. Her legs still wrapped around my waist. I hold onto her hips pulling her into me harder than before. I could feel how the tip of my dick hit her sweet spot every time. Her walls clamp around my dick as she cums all over me, the force of her orgasm sends me over the edge without warning. I spilled my juices inside of her. Both of us moaning the other's name. I brace myself above her so as to not crush her, both of us panting, trying to catch our breath. I stayed like that for a moment, giving her sweet kisses, before laying down next to her. I pull her to my chest, wanting to hold her for a moment.

"That was..." I tense and I am sure she could feel it.

Before she could say anything I spoke up. "That was a mistake... Sorry." I feel her pull away. She grabs her clothes, putting them on faster than anything. "Elena..." I try to reach for her but she pulls away.

"I will get you back to the house." She jumped off the bed of the truck and got behind the wheel. I grab my clothes to put them on. I could see the hurt in her eyes when she got dressed. I am such a jerk. Who says that to someone? But I needed her to know that this couldn't happen again. I guess I could have said it differently.

I get in on the passenger side. "I'm sorry... It came out wrong." She looks at me and nods. I could see the tears in her eyes.

"It's my fault. I knew you were a player. I guess, I am just another notch on your belt." Damn why does that sting so much? I shouldn't have let this go that far. She never deserved to just be a one night thing. She deserves the world.

CHAPTER 7 - ELENA

I am not naive, I knew that sleeping with Mason wouldn't change anything. I mean I didn't expect him to confess his undying love to me, but what he did just ripped my heart out. *"That was a mistake... Sorry."* His words are ringing in my ears. A mistake. I have been called many things but a mistake has never been one of them.

I drive up the driveway at my ranch. I know I said I would sleep over at Jake's. But after what happened, I just want my bed.

Mason still tried to talk to me on the way back to the house. I just didn't want to be reminded of being a mistake. I dropped him off and told him I would see him later. He really is something. Gives a girl the best damn pleasure known to mankind and then shatters her world with one work. *Mistake*.

I make my way up to my bedroom, just wanting to forget the night. Wanting to forget

Mason Ashford. Being hurt by Ben didn't even hurt as much as being called a Mistake hurts. I crawl into bed and cover my face. I will deal with everything in the morning. I will face everyone and anything that is thrown at me.

I woke up the next morning to the sound of Gramps' laughter. He has always been the happy go lucky man he is now. Nothing gets him down. He also always sees the good in people, no matter what they do wrong. So if Gramps don't like you, it means that you are not likeable. I force myself out of bed. Padding over to the bathroom to get ready for the day. I would have to see Mason today even though I don't want to see him. The wedding party is coming over for lunch.

After getting ready I made my way down to the kitchen to see a few of the staff hell Gramps with the lunch preparation. "Morning. Is there something I can do?" Gramps turns around and his smile fades.

"What's wrong sweetheart? I thought you were staying at Jake's!" He pulls me into his arms. I melt into his arms, this is my safe place.

"The party ended early so I decided to come home and help you." I lied. I don't want him to worry about me.

"Whoever he is... He is not worth your tears. If he knows what he has he will kick his own ass for letting a gem like you go." Gramps kisses the top of my head. How does he do it? He knows exactly what to say to make me feel better.

"Who is he? I will kick his ass." John walks in and gives me a kiss on the head. "Morning Gramps." He pats Gramps on the shoulder.

"It's no one. I am just busy with the wedding and all that stuff." I let go of Gramps and walked over to the coffee pot.

"I heard some big shot wants to buy the ranch." John says while he grabs two cups.

"Where did you hear that?" I take the cups and fill them with coffee. John motions for me to follow him. We walk out the back door onto the deck. John takes a seat on one of the lounge chairs and I sit next to him. "There was a guy at the bar last night. His name's Benjamin." I roll my eyes at the mention of his name. "What bothered me was that he was with those ladies you were with. He looked quite cozy with the one."

"He loves cheating on his girl." I say while remembering the way he treated me. How he broke my trust.

"It wasn't just a one night thing. It seemed as if he knew them." I drag my hand through my hair. I need to find out who he was working for. I can't let him take my ranch. I won't sell it to anyone.

John turns to look me in the eyes. "He spoke about a Mason guy." My heart sank just hearing that. "By the look on your face, I take it you know the guy."

"I know him alright. What did he say about Mason?" John shifts on his chair, I could tell he was uncomfortable.

"He told them that Mason fired him after he found out he cheated on his girl. The girls were shocked, then he said he hopes Mason buys the ranch and breaks down everything you have worked for, well he said the owner worked for. This Benjamin guy is pretty pissed at you." I nervously chuckle.

"He was my ex. The one that cheated on me." John sighs and looks out at the mountain. I could see that he is trying to keep himself calm.

"I wanted to say that he looks familiar. I should have kicked his ass last night."

"No... You remember that big company I would have worked for if I didn't leave?" I pull out my phone and go into my emails. I needed to find that email.

"I remember. You gave up everything when that Jerk broke your heart."

"Eh. He was just another one of my many failed relationships." John puts his hand on my arm and shakes his head. I spot the email just as we hear footsteps coming towards us.

"Sorry we are early. We wanted to help Gramps with setting up." I look over my shoulder and my eyes meet the one person I don't want to see right now. I can't even deal with Ben today, but Mason... I can't deal with him. I don't want to deal with him.

John pats my thigh as he gets up. My eyes never leave Mason as his eyes follow every move John makes. His eyes turn a shade darker as he stares at John. "He would be happy with some muscles to help." John walks back into the kitchen. Mason stops before following him. It seems as if he wanted to say something, but stopped himself.

"Mas... Come on." Jake pulls Mason by the shirt. I shake my head. Why did I think he would want to talk to me? I get up from where I am sitting and walk over to the picnic area, where lunch will be served. The things I am feeling right now might just make me want to run away. Ben worked for Mason. Does that mean Mason was the one that wanted to buy my ranch. And if that is true, is that the reason he was flirting with me. Did he think that sleeping with me would make me hand over my ranch to him?

MASON ASHFORD

When I woke up this morning I regretted everything that happened last night. No, that's not true. I regretted everything that happened after we were done fucking. If that is even what I could call it. When we were together it felt right. Like that was where I was supposed to be. Like Elena was what I have been searching for this whole time. It felt right. But once the ecstasy wore off and I came to my senses my insecurity once again took a hold of me. Why would she want to be with me? Does she only see me for my money? All these things went through my mind and when she talked I knew I had to get her to hate me. *"That was a mistake... Sorry."* The words that ripped my heart in two as soon as it left my lips and I saw the hurt in her eyes. But her words broke me more, even more than when Marley told me that she wasn't in love with me. Elena will never talk to me again, not after I called her a *mistake*. Truthfully she was everything but a *mistake*.

I didn't come to the ranch and expected to be knocked off my boots by a down to earth country girl. Yet, here I am still laying in my bed, trying to figure out how to fix this. Having her drive off last night without a smile or a see you soon, has been haunting me the whole night. I lied, that was the most mind blowing sex I have ever had and I have had a lot. She fitted against me like she was made for me. I should have said something else... Literally anything would have worked, anything would have been better than calling her a mistake.

I turn towards my door as it opens. "Hey, get dressed. We are going over to the Monroe ranch. I need to get away from the girls." He stops when he sees my face. "What did you do?" I roll my eyes. Of course it's me that did something.

"Nothing..."

"Mas... I know you. You look as if your heart has been trampled on. Now I know that Elena wouldn't have done anything to hurt you, unless you did something." Jake closes the door and sits down on the edge of my bed.

I push myself up by the elbows and narrow my eyes at Jake. "I might have slept with Elena and then called her a mistake." I huffed before falling onto my pillow again.

"YOU WHAT?" He shouts and I try to shush him. He swats my hand away. "Why would you do that? And don't shush me. I told you she isn't like other girls. She falls and she falls hard. For her to let you in her pants means that she cares more about you than you know." He gets up from my bed pacing the floor. Now I feel even worse than I did. Even though I didn't want to admit it, I am falling for her too. I have been fighting my feelings, but last night almost killed me.

"We had a magical evening. Everything about her is perfect. One thing led to another, after we were done. Both of us laid there in silence until she said that was... I ended up interrupting her by saying that was a mistake... Sorry." I look down at my hands feeling ashamed of myself for the first time in my life. I never cared what anyone thought of me. All I cared about was me and what I wanted. But sitting here and seeing the disappointment in Jake's eyes makes me want to crawl into the nearest whole and stay there. "Once the words left my lips I knew they were wrong, but it was done. She was hurt and she didn't want to talk to me again." Jake stops pacing. He shakes his head in even more disappointment.

"Tell me honestly. Was it a mistake or are you starting to fall for her. Because fuck knows that I have no idea of what the hell is going on with you these last few days." I get up and walk over to where he is standing. I stop right in front of him to make sure he looks into my eyes.

"Honestly, I am… I have been trying to fight the attraction I have towards her. Last night I went in with the idea of just fucking her, but it ended up as more than just a quick fuck and that scared the shit out of me. I thought that we only had a physical attraction and once we had our fill it would be over. But as soon as the words left my lips, I knew that it was more than just sexual, I am slowly falling for my raven haired, blue eyed country girl. The girl that dances to any country song as if no one is watching. The girl that doesn't care what anyone says or thinks of her. The girl that rode in on her horse and stole my heart. The heart I didn't even know could be stolen. And honestly I don't want my heart back, I want my girl back." I could feel the sting in my eyes and I blinked a few times. I couldn't cry in front of Jake and yet there he stood with teary eyes himself.

"I might be a jerk, but I will help you. We have to fix this, because honestly, I have never heard you talk about a girl that way. Not even Marley. You are in love my friend. " Jake pulls me into a hug and I am certain it is only to wipe his eyes.

I pull back from our hug. "I meant every word. I will do anything I can to get her back. I just want a chance to tell her how I feel." Jake nods as he walks to my dresser, he pulls out a shirt and throws it at me.

"Get ready. We will head to the ranch. Just play it cool for now. Give her a moment to cool off. Knowing Elena, if you get there now she might kill you... No, she will definitely kill you" I chuckle as I walk into the bathroom. I hear the door close and know Jake left. Maybe I can fix this whole mess, but how will she feel when I try to take the ranch she works at.

After I got ready, I headed downstairs only to hear Zena and Marley talking. I freeze when I hear them talk about Benjamin and the Monroe Ranch.

"He told me that the owner would never sell." Zena states.

"Mason could convince anyone. Benjamin is just sore because he got fired." I try to take a step closer without them seeing me.

"Well, I know that if Mason doesn't buy the ranch, I am going to get my father to buy it. Maybe then I will get him back." Fuck, I can't let Zena do that.

"I like that idea. What I heard was that Elena works on the ranch. You could get the ranch, the man and put her out on her ass." Marley's voice made me sick. She makes me sick. I can't believe I was ready to give up love because of what she did to me. I am just glad that Elena was able to break down my walls.

"What are you doing?" Jake talks next to me and scares the shit out of me. I turn around to motion to the door that leads to the living room.

"Listen."

"I don't know. She is a good worker. I might just flaunt my relationship with Mason in front of her." Jake grabs my arm and I swear I can see the smoke coming out of his ears.

"I just want her gone. I hate that she is around Mason. It is like she has a spell on him and he is like a lost puppy that follows her around everywhere. I can't stand her." Jake shakes his head and I can see the hurt in his eyes. He pulls me to the other side and I follow him. We go out through the back door.

"Jake..." He turns and looks at me. I could see my friend breaking right in front of me. He was getting married in a few days and it was as if he didn't even know his soon to be wife.

"I can't... She hates Elena near you. Why does she care?"

"I don't know what to say. All I do know is that she changed." I had no words for Jake right now. The way she was acting was not the Marley that I met. This Marley is manipulative and bitchy.

"Let's go. I need to cool down." We head to the truck and get into the truck. The ride over to the Monroe ranch is quiet and I am sure that Jake has a million thoughts running through his head. I will be there for him, but I will not tell him what to do. This has to be his choice. He is the one that needs to live with her for the rest of his life.

Jake parks near the front of the mansion and we walk to the back after one of the workers said that Gramps is at the back. "You know this ranch?" I ask as I look around.

"Yes, I spend a lot of time here." We walk onto the deck by the back door and that is when I see her. Her blue eyes sparkle with unshed tears as she stares at me. My eyes follow every move the guy next to her makes. The way his hand touches her thigh, not even 24 hours ago my hand was on her thigh. Was she playing me? Was I a joke to her? My eyes lock on hers again as the guy walks past me. No, she wouldn't have been this broken about what I said if she was playing me. This guy was just comforting her. I am about to say something to her when Jake's pulls me away from her and into the mansion.

"Not now. She's hurt." He pulls me with him. "Let me introduce you. This is John, a friend of ours." He motions to the guy that was just with Elena.

"Well, aren't you handsome?" He winks at me and I feel like kicking myself for doubting Elena.

"It's nice to meet you. I'm Mason." John's eyes grow wide as he looks from me to Jake. I instantly know something is wrong.

"I am sorry. I have to go." He takes a step closer to me. "If you hurt Elena in any way. They will never find your body. This ranch is big and I will help her hide the body." He pushes past me and I have no idea what he was talking about. Maybe he knows about last night, but he wouldn't have reacted that way. It has to be something else... And then it hits me... Benjamin!

CHAPTER 8 - MASON

Jake and I help Gramps carry a few things around while the staff and Elena set up the tables. I watch her as she dances around John and he just laughs at her moving around to the beat of some country song.

"You better watch out... You have a little drool." Gramps goes to wipe my chin and I gently swat his hand away. Was I that obvious? He considers me for a moment. "Have you gotten to know her? Like really know her?" I turn my attention to the old man.

"I think I have. I spent every day with her and we talked about everything and anything." He nods as he takes in what I am saying. "She has this way that she scrunches up her nose when she is deep in thought. When she gets really excited her eyes turn icy blue and sparkle more than before. She hates it when people look down on others and money doesn't bother her in the faintest. To her everyone is the same." He smiles as he listens. "When the light catches her hair at the right moment it almost looks purple. She's a raven beauty with a heart of gold that would do anything for anyone." He places his hand on my shoulder and looks between me and her.

"You say all the right things and yet you still broke her heart." I stood there shocked. How the hell did he know? Did Elena really tell her boss what she did last night?

"I'm sorry?" He shakes his head disappointed with my answer or rather question.

"She didn't have to say anything. I saw it in her eyes. You don't know her as you say you do. All those things you mentioned are when she's happy. But look at her now..." He points over to Elena and John. "What do you see?"

I turn to really look at her. I feel my eyes well up in realization that I did this. This is all my fault. "She's hurting. The sparkle in her eyes isn't there. Her smile never meets her eyes. She's laughing, but there is a sadness to it." He nods. "She not once meets anyone's eyes. How can I fix it?"

"Figure out what you did to break her. You can't fix something, before you haven't figured out how it broke." He narrows his eyes at me. "You did her worse than what Ben did. I can tell. She wasn't this broken after she broke up with Ben."

"I will do what I have to, to fix this." Jake pops up next to me with this heart warming smile and it freaks me the fuck out. "Don't do that, you look way too creepy."

He wiggles his eyebrows. "I know how you can start to win her over. " I give him my full attention.

"Well... Are you going to tell me?" Gramps walks over to the radio and changes the song. I look at Jake with dread in my eyes. I would rather sing than dance.

"Grab her and dance with her. I will make sure her favorite song comes up."

"And that is..." I ask as he pushes me towards Elena. John shakes his head as Gramps and Jake shows him to walk away. He obviously knows the whole story. I mean he made it clear in the kitchen.

"Knocking boots...." Jake yells as he goes over to where Gramps was standing. They fumble with the radio for a few minutes as I try and take my time walking over to Elena. She's standing with her back towards me. I hope that she will give me a chance to do this. I need her to smile and at least have a bit of fun. Real fun.

An upbeat country song comes on over the speakers and I see Elena's eyes light up. She starts to sway her hips from side to side as her hands go into her hair. I take that as my chance to wrap my arms around her waist pulling her against my chest.

"What are you doing?" She tries to push away from me, but I start to move around the table with her in my arms.

"Just go with the music." I whisper into her ear. She looks up at me for a brief moment and I can still see the hurt in her eyes. She hangs on to me as we move to the music. I feel her body relax as we dance, I grab her hand and spin her out before I pull her back into me. She lets out a genuine throaty laugh as she hits my chest again. The sparkle in her eyes almost back. She rests her head on my chest as I hold her one hand in mine and my other hand rests on the small of her back. I lay my head on top of her head. This right here felt right. Her in my arms. Why did I have to question everything?

The song came to an end, but I didn't want to let her go and it felt as if she didn't want to let me go either. "I'm so sorry..." I whisper in her hair. She tightens the arm she had around my waist, before she let's go of me all of a sudden.

"Thank you for the dance." She turned to walk away, but I kept her hand in mine. She turns around and stares at me. Her blue eyes turn a few shades darker.

"Please... Talk to me." I plead with her and she just shakes her head as she narrows her eyes at me even more.

She points her finger at me. "You want to talk... Let's talk.." She jabs her finger into my chest. "Did Benjamin work for you?" She spits out and I freeze. How does she know that?

"Elena, please I can..."

"Don't even dare come up with a lame excuse. You send your lawyer to come and make an offer on my ranch. And when I didn't accept, you decided to make me fall for you and then told me that I am a mistake..." She slams her tiny fists into my chest and I see her eyes welling up. Her ranch...

"I'm sorry for last night..." I try to get her to listen to me but she just looks at me with so much hate in her eyes.

"You're not sorry. You are sorry you got caught. This is my ranch... I will never sell it. You are welcome here only when you are here with Jake. After lunch today, I don't want to see you on *MY Property* ever again." She turns around and walks off. Jake runs over to me and stares at me with even more disappointment.

"How could you? This place means everything to her. This is all she has left of her parents."

"Jake..." He just shakes his head running after her. I am going to kill Benjamin. He had to open his mouth. But how did she find out?

Gramps stood next to me. He puts his hand on my shoulder.

"You didn't know the ranch belonged to her, did you?"

"No, I thought you were the owner and that she was only working here." Gramps nods in understanding. I should have known better than to assume. She always said that money didn't bother her. She never corrected anyone that brought her down and she didn't flaunt it that she owned a ranch. That's just not who she is.

"Give her some time. She will talk to you when she's ready. For now, she just found out that you plan to take her ranch and she's not happy." He walks off leaving me there to wallow in my own sorrow. I turn and walk over to where the grass meets the stream running through the property. I needed a moment to collect my thoughts, I needed to get her to listen to me. She needs to know that I would never just take her property from her. If she ended up telling me no, I would have just let it go.

I have been fighting my feelings since I met Elena and now that I am ready to give in, this obstacle gets in our way. If only Benjamin had left like I told him to leave. Then she wouldn't have known that he worked for me and that I was planning on buying the ranch if he just left.

"I know you want to be alone..." A voice startled me. I turn around and see John standing there. "I was the one that told her about Ben working for you. I was the one that picked up the pieces when she left him." He picks up a pebble and throws it across the stream. "When she came back she focused all her time on the ranch. She wasn't broken, she said she knew they were over a while ago, she just hoped that they could work things out." He turns to look at me. "But when I saw her this morning, I got scared. She looked broken the way she looked when she lost her parents. I was scared of losing my best friend. I told her what I heard Ben say. That he was working for you and that you would do what you could to take this ranch." I stood there listening with my hands in my pocket.

"I never said I would do what I could to take the ranch. Why would you say that?"

"Because that is what Ben said. He said that you wanted the ranch no matter what it took. He also said you fired him, but asked him to come back to help you with the deal. That you would do anything to take the ranch." I could feel the anger burning inside of me. That dick thinks he can get away with this.

"I never said that. I would never bully anyone into selling their property. I have morals. I also didn't ask him to come back." John looked at me confused. I had to find out what was going on. I need to make sure that Elena doesn't lose the ranch. She might hate me now. But I will make sure that I prove to her who I really am and that I never wanted to hurt her.

CHAPTER 9 - ELENA

Dancing with Mason was the best feeling in the world. I almost forgot about what he did. It felt real... Like I was meant to be in his arms. I felt free as he spins me out and pulled me back into his arms. I could hear his heart beat when I laid my head on his chest, it was almost as if it was beating to the beat of the music. I felt my heart flutter when he whispered he was sorry into my hair, but then I remembered that Ben worked for him. That he wants to take my ranch from. That he only gave me the time of day, because he thought if he softened me up I would give him the ranch. I am not going to fall for that. I knew he was out of my league and yet I still went and fell for him.

I walk towards the house, when I see Marley and Zena get out of a car with Alex and Penny right behind them. I can't deal with all of them right now. I know I have too, but I can't.

"El..." I hear Jake call me. I stop and wait for him to catch up to me. "Are you alright?" He asks when he gets next to me.

"I am fine..." I start to slowly walk to the other side of the mansion where there is a big swing in one of the trees. "Do you remember that one summer we got into trouble because of this swing?" Jake chuckles as I take a seat and he starts pushing me on the swing.

"How could I forget? I wasn't allowed to see you for a whole week. Your mom believed that I was the one to talk you into swinging that high and jumping off. You almost broke your neck" I laugh the higher I go. Up here I feel free, like nothing could get to me.

"In all fairness, you did dare me to do it."

"I know, but I still didn't think you would go that high." He stops the swing and kneels down in front of me. "Mason is a good guy. I don't know the whole story, but I am sure he would tell you if you asked him." I could only nod. There is one thing I want to know and I hope that Jake could answer.

"Can I ask you something? And I want you to be totally honest with me. I know that Mason is your friend, but so am I." Jake takes my hands in his giving them a little squeeze

"You know you can ask me anything and I will always be honest with you." This is still the Jake that I know. He has not changed much in the last few years.

"Did Mason know that I am the owner of the ranch?"

"I don't think so. He never said anything about it. He did ask me about the ranch and you and I never told him that you are the owner and from what I understood. He thought you only worked here. Why?"

I pull my hands out of his. If Mason didn't know then everything he said and done the past few days has been true. Do I want it to be true and feel heartbroken that I was a mistake... But then again he did say he was sorry. Why isn't it ever easy. A girl falls in love and the guy also falls in love and they live happily ever after.

"Elena... Why do you ask?" Damn I was so deep in my own head, I have no idea how long I have been staring at him.

"I was wondering if he used me. If everything he did was to get me to sign over the ranch to him." I look down at my hands as Jake lets out a loud sigh.

"Look Elena, I get it. Mason might be an ass, but he would never do something like that. Everything he did the last few days was because he wanted to. Not because he is some manipulative man. He is my best friend, just like you. He would never do what you think he did." I felt the tears sting my eyes. I feel so embarrassed that I even thought that he would do that. I wanted a reason to hate him after what he did last night, and yet there is no reason.

I throw my arms around Jake's neck and give him a hug. "Thank you Jake. I guess I shouldn't just jump to conclusions."

"No, you shouldn't. Let's get to this lunch that Gramps prepared for us." He gets up and holds his arm out for me. I link my arm with his as we start to walk towards the area the picnic is being held.

As we get closer to the group I see Zena next to Mason. They are talking, but she runs her hand up and down his chest. I wanted to talk to him, but it will have to wait. His attention is on his friends right now.

"As if leading on my friend wasn't enough, now you have to actually try and steal my fiance." Marley pulls my arm away from Jake and pushes me to the side. "Go do whatever it is you do around here. This is only for the owner and the wedding party. And guess what, you aren't invited." Gramps stands there with a smirk on his face as I just stare at Marley. None of them know that I own the ranch. Why wouldn't Ben tell them?

I step towards the tables. Just as I am about to sit down Zena blocks my path. "This is mine and Mason's seat. Why don't you join the other staff?" She grabs Mason's hand to make him sit next to her. I was about to say something when John called out to me.

"El... Come sit here with us." He glares at Zena and Mason. After what Jake told me about Mason, I can't be upset with him. I was the one that thought the worst of him. Mason locked eyes with me and all I could do was give him a faint smile.

"Could you just leave. You are ruining my fucking wedding bitch." I turn to see Marley storm towards me. I don't have time to move out of the way. She tackles me to the ground and pins my shoulders on the ground. "Mason wasn't enough... You had to sink your claws into Jake. I will make you regret the day you were born." Marley lifts her fist to hit me, but she gets pulled off of me. "Let me go...." She fights against the arm around her shoulder.

Mason kneels next to me. "What can I do?" I look up at him.

"I'm alright. She didn't hurt me." He holds out his hand to help me up. I look at it and just as I am about to take it. Zena appears behind him taking his hand that he was offering me in hers.

"Mas... We have a problem." She pulls him away from me. I huff and look at them walking towards Jake and Marley.

"Damn girl, what the hell did you do?" Alex holds his hand out to me, I take it and he helps me up. I brush the dust and grass off my jeans. "What do you think happened?" I stand next to him watching the scene unfold in front of me. Jake waves his hands around and Mason stands next to him, with his arms crossed over his chest looking damn sexy as hell. Zena comforts Marley as she cries and pleads with Jake. He shakes his head and throws his hands in the air. They are just too far for us to hear what is going on.

"By the way... I didn't do anything. Miss possessive just tackled me." Alex chuckles, never taking his eyes off the fighting couple. Mason smirks and looks in our direction. "It looks serious..."

"Yes, Jake looks upset." I try to think back at what could have happened. Shit, is this because Jake talked to me before they arrived? "Jake was with you when we got here. Did he say anything?"

"No, we were talking about Mason. Then Marley showed up and started shouting at me. She and Jake stayed to talk. That's all I know." Alex glances at me, but both our attention goes back to Jake and Marley when we hear the slap. "Shit, what just happened?"

Marley throws her ring in Jake's face and walks away with Zena following her. Jake turns away from Mason. Alex and I make our way over to Jake and Mason.

"Not now guys." Mason whispers.

"We will get lunch served. Take your time." Mason grabs my hand, giving it a little squeeze.

"Thanks. We will be there as soon as he is up to it." Mason gives me a kiss on the cheek and for some reason I don't pull away. Maybe we could have a civil conversation and we can work out these feelings we have.

I turn to walk back to the tables with Alex, but Jake's voice stops me in my tracks. "The wedding is off." He says in a hoarse voice. I look over my shoulder. Just to see that he hasn't turned around or even moved from where he is standing.

"Is there anything we can do for you?" Jake lets out a hollow laugh.

"Can I stay here tonight... Please. I can't face everyone right now." My heart breaks for my friend.

I glance at Mason to try and find out what I should do. I would let Jake stay here without another thought. But he did just call off the wedding, I don't want to cause more problems for him. Mason nods his head agreeing with Jake.

"Sure, you know you are always welcome here. I will ask them to get your room ready for you."

"I would also like to stay, please." I smile.

"I will get the rooms ready. Alex?" He looks between me and Mason.

His eyes go wide. "Yes please. No way I am staying at the house with the girls. They will skin me alive or worse sacrifice me just to put a spell on Jake or on you. Nope... I am staying right here." Jake chuckles and turns around to look at us all.

"Alex, only you could make me laugh after calling off my wedding." Wait... What? Jake called off the wedding. Why would he do that?

I think Alex was just as shocked as I was. "Jake... You called it off?" Alex says just above a whisper.

"I did. I couldn't stand her attitude anymore. Also I found something out this morning." He looks towards Mason. "I can't marry someone that only wants to break other people down." Mason puts his hand on Jake's shoulder.

I shake my head. I feel he made a rash decision. "Jake, are you sure? I mean she could just be stressed because of the wedding." Jake shakes his head as does Mason.

"She's not. She cheated on me with fucking Benjamin." He runs his hand through his hair. I have absolutely no idea what to say to them. I know how it feels to be cheated on.

"Wait, so that means she has been with Benjamin even before she told you that she wanted to be with Jake?" Mason nods. I could see the hurt in his eyes.

"How did you find out?" Alex questions.

Jake pulls out his phone. "After you left to come back to the tables I received this message. It had photos attached. The things they did made me sick." Jake holds his phone out to us. I wave my hand dismissing the phone.

"No thanks. I will take your word for it." I take a few steps towards him. "I am sorry this had to happen to both of you. Benjamin is a womanizer and he loves to break up happy relationships." Mason shakes his head.

"No, you can only seduce the other person if they want to be seduced. If she was invested in this relationship, then she wouldn't have fucked him time and time again." Mason's voice is low and full of hate. "I can't believe I never saw it. Whenever we went to L.A she always stayed in the hotel when I had to go out to my meetings. It never bothered me, I thought she just didn't want to intrude on my meetings." He brushes his hand down his face. I wanted to give him a hug, but now was not the right time. "What hurts is that she hurt me and also hurt my best friend days before the wedding." Jake pats Mason's back as they share a look.

"It's days like this, that I wish you never hired Benjamin. That your first lawyer never left." Jake huffs out.

"What do you mean never hired Benjamin. Who were you going to hire in the first place?" I was all giddy inside right now. Was it Mason that was supposed to be my boss?

"I am not sure... It was a girl. I have the documents at my office. She was the best candidate for what I wanted, but when I got there I was informed that she left and wasn't coming back. They explained to me that Benjamin worked closely with her and he might be the second best option." I feel my blood boil as Mason explains. I know exactly what happened. I was the one that left. I was the one that told my boss to give my accounts to Benjamin.

"Fuck.... He played me ...." Jake lifts his head looking at me like a light bulb has just come on.

"It was you..." Jake says as he points to me.

"Yes... I was so excited about working for Ashford hotels. Why didn't I put two and two together? He kept telling me that the account was too big for me, I should either share or let him take over..."

"Fuck..." Mason interrupts me. "This makes sense. Marley wasn't happy with my choice. She told me that a woman won't be able to handle the pressure that comes with our industry." I laugh... Tears were streaming down my face as I laughed. Marley surely doesn't know me. I run a whole ranch, nothing scares me.

"He planned it. He knew that if he broke my heart I would leave and come back here. He didn't know why, but he knew I wouldn't stay and that I would just hand over my accounts to him." Do I feel stupid right now... Yes. The jerk planned everything. He took the one account that I actually really wanted. Am I regretting coming home and building my life here? No... My life is what I want it to be. But I could have had Mason as my boss and still have had all this.

Mason walks away from us. "Mas..." He holds up his hand and Jake stops talking.

"I just need a minute. I just have to wrap my head around this." We all stayed back to give him his time. I smirk at Jake and he gives me a smirk right back. It's payback time. Marley and Ben have probably been planning this for a long time. We just need to find out why. What do they want to achieve?

My worst fear is that they plan to bring Mason down. That they want to hurt him for some reason. I wouldn't be able to sit back and let them do it.

CHAPTER 10 - MASON

Hearing everything that happened. How Marley manipulated us. She almost made me lose my best friend and for what. Some kind of vendetta she has. I had to find out how deep this goes. She surely has a plan. There's a reason why she wanted to marry Jake. Why she still saw Benjamin or Ben like Elena calls him. Fuck... Elena, she is as much a victim here as us. Ben used her, took the account she was meant to have. He took my account. I was supposed to have met her the day I met Ben. But then again, that time I was in love with Marley, I wouldn't have even glanced at her. I believe the saying, everything happens for a reason. I just have to find that reason.

I just needed a minute. I just needed to calm myself down. Hearing Marley tell Jake all the things she did after he showed her the photos, it almost broke me. She confessed to never loving me. She told him that she would make sure I am never happy. She just doesn't know that I heard her. That I was there when she told him that she thought of Ben every time we fucked. I have to be honest, that stung a bit. I gave her everything. I gave her my heart and she took it and stomped on it. What is worse is that I almost gave her the power over me. After her I wanted to give up on love, but guess fate had another plan. It wanted me to meet the Raven beauty dressed in cowboy boots and a cowboy hat, the raven beauty with the most striking blue eyes. Just thinking of the fact that I almost lost her, I almost blew everything because of my insecurities.

I have to go back to her and tell her about my plans. I have to tell her why I wanted to buy her ranch. But most of all I have to tell her how I feel about her. That this was all real for me even though I tried to fight it the best I could. If after everything she still doesn't want to be with me, I will respect that and hope that we will still be able to be friends.

The sky has turned dark, I have no idea how long I have been out here. I missed the whole lunch. But then again it wasn't a wedding lunch anymore. I turn to go back only to discover that I have absolutely no idea where the hell I am.

"Great Mason. Get lost and die on the night you find out your ex girlfriend is a lying cheating bitch that wants to make your life hell." I mutter to myself as I try to find any sign of where I am. "As if there are going to be road signs or any signs pointing you in the direction of the ranch house." I shake my head walking back the way I came. It would lead me somewhere right. I know that if I can find a fence I could follow it. It should lead me somewhere.

I walk for a bit, before I notice that I am really lost. "Note to self. Don't go walking on a ranch you don't know, especially if you are deep in thought, fighting with your demons." I let out a frustrated sigh. I know that someone will come looking for me. Maybe I should just wait. But then again that is not me. I don't sit around and wait for people to do things. I need to find my own way out of this.

"My phone..." I could kick myself for not thinking of that the first time. I could call someone and ask them to send me a location. Then I could use my GPS and get back without anyone having to come out and look for me.

I pull out my phone seeing that my battery is low. I pray that it will last for me to at least get back to the main house.

I dial Jake's number and it just rings and rings. Great, my best friend ignores me the day that I really need him. I dial Elena's number and a man answers her phone. I feel a tad bit jealous, but I have to get over that for now.

"Hello..."

"Hi, is Elena there?" I ask in a hurry. My battery might die any minute.

I hear the guy let out a sigh. "No, she's out looking for you." He sounds a bit irritated. But I only heard that she's out looking for me. She cares enough to come look for me. "Mason... Hello..."

"Yeah, sorry. Could you send me a location? Maybe I could find my way back." I take my phone away to check my battery.

"No, send me your location. I will send them out to you. It will be safer that way." I didn't know why, but I felt as if something wasn't right.

"Sure. That might be better. My battery is about to die."

"Alright. Send it and hang tight. They will come find you. You have been gone for hours." I hear a commotion in the background. I could hear Jake and someone else shouting.

"What's happening there?" It's quiet for a moment. "Is everyone alright?" Still the guy doesn't come back. The shouting got louder and then the line went dead. What the hell was that? Who did I just talk to? Jake seemed upset and he was calling for Elena?

I had to find my way back there and I had to do it on my own. I go into my gps and type in Monroe ranch. Hopefully it would at least take me to the main gate. And it did. It showed me the way to the main gate. I took off running in the direction of the main gate. The woods were dark with only the light of the moon lighting up the path. I didn't care about the dangers around me, I had a feeling that Elena and Jake were in trouble and that they needed me. I would call the police once I get to the main road. I wouldn't need my phone anymore from there.

ELENA TATE

After we watched Mason walk off we went back to the guest. Jake didn't feel like getting into anything and asked me to just tell them to enjoy the lunch and that they will be informed of the proceedings within the next few hours. And that is what I did. I told him that the room he always used is ready and he could just go there if he wanted to. But he wanted to go to the one place he always found peace, it's a small pond between a wall of trees. We have always tried to find out how the water got there. The pond always has water and it's always sparkling blue. There is a big flat rock on the one side and Jake normally sits under that rock not to be disturbed, Bot that anyone knows about the pond. It's the spot he went to when his dad died.

"Thank you all for coming. Jake and Marley will not be joining us for lunch. Jake asks that you all enjoy the lunch. He will let you all know the proceedings for the rest of the week a bit later. Please help yourself to the lunch spread, done by my grandpa." I wave my hand in the direction of the food. Everyone nods as they walk over to help themselves.

"What happened?" I turn to see Mrs. Forester standing behind me. I can't tell her. It's not my place to deliver the news. "Listen, I know the wedding's off. Marley rushed into the house shouting and throwing things around. She said she will make Jake and Mason pay. They will never get away with this." I gave her a small smile.

"Mrs. Forester, I can't tell you. It's not my place. All I can say is that things aren't always as they seem. Marley isn't who Jake thought she was. He is hurt, but he will be alright." I put my hand on her arm to try and reassure her that Jake is doing alright.

"What about Mason?" I was shocked she asked and I am sure she saw it on my face. "He is like my son. I am worried about him."

"He needed a minute. I am sure he will also be fine once this is all over." She nods before she gives me a quick hug. She walks back to the table and John and Alex appear next to me.

"Let's go eat. We are going to need our strength." John points to the one side where Ben is standing against the wall talking and flirting to Penny. Poor girl, if only she knew. I could go over there and tell him to leave my property, but I think we all had enough drama for a day. If he doesn't cause any trouble, I will let him stay for the time being. But he has to leave when everyone else leaves.

"I am going to see if I can find anything out." John chirps as he walks away towards Ben even before I was able to stop him. Dammit my stubborn gay best friend. He doesn't know when to leave it alone.

"He is going to get into trouble." All I could do was shake my head agreeing with him. "How are you holding up? I mean you, Jake and Mason found out you have all been played and yet you are the only one that didn't run in a direction wanting a minute to yourself." I glance up at Alex. He has been so sweet since I met him. He is almost like the big brother I never thought I wanted.

"I am alright. The difference is that I knew Ben wasn't the one for me. Whereas Mason gave his everything to Marley and she broke his heart not once but twice. And Jake was ready to spend the rest of his life with her only to find out she has been sleeping with another guy since being with Mason. They both got pretty badly hurt in a short period of time. So I am fine. I will be strong for the three of us, until they are able to be strong again." Alex throws his arm around my shoulders. He smiles down at me. His brown hazel eyes shining with adoration.

"You are something else Elena Tate. Other girls would be sitting in a corner crying themselves to sleep, but not you. Here you are taking charge to give your best friend and can I say lover a chance to heal themselves. Here you are being strong for two men, because they mean everything to you." I feel my eyes well up hearing how Alex saw this. "They are extremely lucky to have you on their side. Ben and Marley don't know what they lost. Ben lost a diamond the day he decided to play you and cheat on you." He kissed the top of my head, before he walked over to the lunch table. I follow him, not sure if I will be able to eat something.

After everyone was done and started leaving, John, Alex and I started helping Gramps clear the area. The sun was slowly setting and I started to worry about Mason and Jake. I knew that Jake would find his way back, but Mason doesn't know the ranch.

"They will be back." Gramps says as he carries the one dish inside. I follow behind him with my own dish.

"Jake will, but Mason doesn't know the area. What if he gets lost or even worse gets hurt." Alex walks in with a look on his face that says he is about to kill someone. "What is it?"

He nods to the door with his head. I walk over to see Ben standing at the door with a smirk on his face.

"I waited for everyone to leave." I folded my arms over my chest waiting for him to enlighten me to why he is on my property. "I have documents for you and I would suggest you sign them. It's a really good offer." He holds the documents out to me. Gramps works at the counter, but Alex and John lean over my shoulder to see what is on the paper.

I take it out and my eyes widen. "You're kidding right?" He gives me a devilish smile. "I won't sign. There is no way you are making me sign."

"Elena, that is a good offer. If not, accidents tend to happen when they are not expected." I hand the documents to John, taking a step closer to Ben.

"You do know I am also a lawyer, probably a better one than you. You just threatened me. I am not selling my ranch. So go back to your boss and tell him to go fuck himself. This is my ranch and no one will take it away from me." He laughs in my face before he grabs me around the throat. Before John or Alex could do anything they were hit over the head by two other men.

"You should have taken the deal. But this is fun as well." He pulls me inside and closes the door. Why did I have to let the staff go home for the rest of the day? My only hope would be that Jake and Mason get back here before Ben does something. Why do they want this ranch so badly? There's so many others that's for sale, why want something that isn't for sale.

CHAPTER 11 - ELENA

Ben dragged me towards my room. I have to get out of here, I don't even know what they were doing to Gramps, John and Alex. Truthfully I never even knew that Ben had this evil side.

"Why are you doing this?" I tried to fight against him but he just pushed me into the room.

"You ruined everything. All you had to do was leave and not pop up again. But no, you had to make Mason see you. You had to get him to fall for you." He swirls the gun in his hand around as he paces up and down in front of me. Did he just say that Mason was falling for me? I have to get out of her and find out from Mason. We need to fix this. I want to have a chance to tell him how I feel. I want to have a chance to see where this could go.

"I didn't even know who he was the day I met him. Don't you think that Marley ruined everything. Why didn't she stay with Mason? Why get married to Jake?" Ben starts laughing as he takes something out of his pocket. I moved away from him.

"You are so naive, you have no idea what you have here do you?" He spins in a circle with his arms stretched out. I have to get him talking. I need to know what their plan was from the start.

"I have my family ranch..." I state with confidence. Time to put on my big girl pants and get information. "Why don't you tell me why you are doing this?"

He gives me a mischievous smile and I feel the dread pool in the pit of my stomach. Nothing good can come from the look in his eyes right now. I have to keep him talking long enough for Jake to come back, or Mason to magically appear from his little hike in the woods.

"You know what... I am going to tell you everything because you are not walking out of here." I swallow at his words. He wouldn't really stoop that low and kill me would he.

"If something happens to me, you will never get your hands on the ranch." I could feel the fear wanting to take over. I could take him on, but he could shoot me then. I have to keep him talking.

He pulls one of my chairs closer. "Take a seat on the bed, baby." I feel the bile rising in my throat at the pet name he gives me. I hate the word Baby and it's all because of him. I do as he says. "Now, let's start from the beginning. You see, meeting you was all planned. I knew where you would be and when. I have been watching you for a while. When we started dating, Marley was already busy getting Mason to notice her. And he fell right into her trap. The thing was, Mason wanted love... He has always been the romantic one. Our true victim was Jake... But he was the broody one, never even glancing at Marley, not until Mason asked him to please watch out for her when he wasn't there. Marley took that as the opportunity to get Jake on her side. So I had you and Marley had Jake and Mason wrapped around her finger. Mason left for two months and we knew that it was the time to put our plan into action. First we just wanted Jake, you were collateral. We knew that Ashford Hotels has been watching you since the day you started your Law degree. They wanted you from the start, That is why you were my ticket in with them." He stares at the wall behind me with this proud smile.

"While all this was going on, you slept with Marley?" I had to know if he had her while he was with me.

"Of course. She's my wife..." I choke on my own spit at his words. This fucker had a wife all along and he was sleeping with me. "I know what you're thinking. And yes, I loved fucking you. I have to say you are almost better than Marley, but she is my everything. You were just a means to an end. A good lay for the time I needed you." He gets up and walks over to me. He runs his hand along my cheek and I slaps his hand away.

"Don't touch me...." I spit out. He chuckles and sits down again. "Fine, you wanted Mason and Jake for some reason. What does all of this have to do with my ranch?"

"I was getting to that. So Marley played Jake and Mason. She got Jake to propose to her and she accepted. All they had to do was get married on Saturday, but no... Someone had to send him photos of us together." He gets up and stalks over to me again. Damn I am getting tired of this. I still don't know what this has to do with me and the ranch. "Our whole plan started when we found out that the Monroe Ranch and the Forester Ranch has one of the largest gold reefs running through them. Of course we knew that Jake was the heir to the Forester Ranch, that was the reason Marley wanted to marry him and then his whole family would have died in a plane accident along with Mason. We didn't know who the Monroe Ranch's owner was, all I knew at the time was that an old man was seeing working here. Imagine my surprise when Mason phoned me and told me he wanted to buy the ranch. I thought the old man would sell it to Mason and I made sure that in the contract it stated that I would inherit the ranch if he were to die." I can't believe this. They want to tear my ranch apart in hope to find some gold. "Again imagine my surprise when I saw you on the other side of the door that morning, and finding out all this belongs to you. It made everything easier."

"You plan to kill us all and take the ranches and all that for a little bit of gold?" I shake my head.

"Kill you all, yes... But it is billions of dollars worth of gold...." Ben stops talking when we hear the commotion coming from down stairs... Then I hear his voice.

"Elena...." Jake shouts. Ben glares at me, before he throws something on me. I try to wipe it off but it is sticky.

"Sorry, this is where we say goodbye." He opens the window. I stare at the window as I see some bees flying in. I thought bees sleep at night. And there wasn't supposed to be any on the ranch, everyone knows I am deathly allergic to bees. Ben runs out the door and locks it from the outside.

"Shit..." I get up and run to the bathroom. Three bees were able to sting me before I could close the door. I grabbed the face cloth and wiped the stick residue off me. I feel the tingling in my throat and my tongue. I don't have much time. I need to get my medication and Epi-pen. It should help till I am able to get to the hospital. I have never been stung by three bees at the same time.

I open the medicine cabinet only to find that my Epi-pen isn't in there. "No.... No.... It has to..." I feel the panic rise as breathing becomes difficult.

I hear my bedroom door being kicked open. "Elena... Where are you?" That's Mason... It was my last thought before everything went black.

CHAPTER 12 - MASON

I made my way through the woods and arrived at the main gate. I have never been this scared in my life. I have no idea what was happening in the house, all I know is that they might be in danger.

I dial 911 while I run towards the main house. "911 what's your emergency?" I hear the operator answer.

"My name is Mason Ashford. I need assistants at the Monroe Ranch." I say breathing heavily. I hear the operator typing something.

"Sir, I have dispatched some units. Can you tell me what is going on?" How do I tell her I don't know? She will laugh and call them back.

"Someone is holding the owners hostage." Might be a lie and I will deal with it if they get here and nothing is wrong.

"Where are you sir? And what are you doing?" She asks suspiciously. I swallow, before taking a deep breath.

"I am running towards the house. I took a walk and when I phoned, some guy answered and then there was a lot of commotion... Just send someone. Might want to send an ambulance." I picked up the pace when I saw the lights of the house come nearer.

"They are on their way. Please don't go in. The officers are close." She pleads with me.

"I have to... My girl is in trouble." I put my phone on the table on the porch and slowly make my way to one of the windows. I could see Jake hit a guy and the guys falling to the ground. Gramps, John and Alex were tied on chairs. I lightly knocked on the door. "Jake..." I say just above a whisper making sure he would hear me.

He runs over to the door and opens it. "It's about time you showed up. I will get them untied. Ben dragged Elena up to her room. I will be there in a minute." I didn't even reply. I just dashed up the stairs, but as soon as I got to the top I remembered that I have no idea which room is hers. There were four rooms on this level and three more on the next level. I There were four rooms on this level and three more on the next level. I looked from left to right when John and Jake appeared at the bottom of the stairs.

"The room to your right at the end of the hall." I nodded and ran down the hall towards the room. I tried the door only to find it's locked. I bang on the door but didn't hear anything.

"Break down the door. She might be hurt." Jake says huffing a bit trying to catch his breath. I rammed the door with my shoulder a few times, but it didn't budge. "Let's kick it at the same time." I nod. Jake and I get ready to kick it. It took us two kicks to finally get it opened.

"Damn, I need locks like this." We walk in and I don't see her anywhere. "Elena…. Where are you?" I call out and the only sound I hear is Jake gasping.

"Mas… She is deathly allergic to bees." For the first time I noticed the bees in the room. My eyes land on the closed bathroom door. I am praying with everything in me that she made it to the bathroom without being stung.

I swat Jake's arm. "In there…" I point to the closed door. We both rush over to the door. I bang a few times. "Elena… Open up sweetheart." Nothing, not even a peep. I bang again… Still nothing.

"Get in there. I am going to get her a spare Epi-pen." Jake runs out of the room. If I didn't know that they have been friends for years, I would have been worried. I should have known stuff like this. Yes, I have only known her for a little more than a week. But this is important. I need to make sure if things work out, that I have medication for her. I will have them all over my office, my house and here. She needs to have them everywhere. Some bee is not taking her away from me.

I kick the door open only. I move in and find Elena laying near the bath. I fall to my knees next to her, taking her head and putting it in my lap. Her breathing was shallow and her pulse was weak. I needed to get her help. "Baby, please hang on. There is so much I need to tell you. Please don't give up on me." I lean down and kiss the top of her head just as I hear Jake coming back.

"Move…" I move back a bit as he falls to his knees next to her. He pulls her jeans down to expose her thigh. "She needs this. Don't look at me like that." I nod. I know I was giving him the death glare, but I also know that he knows what he is doing. He sticks the needle into her upper thigh. She gasps and Jake looks up at me. "She needs to get to a hospital. This just gives her a bit of time when it's this excessive. She needs a doctor." Jake states as he pulls her jeans back up.

"Go get the truck ready." He nods and gets up. I move to pick her up. She whimpers as she lays her head against my chest. "Shhh… I got you. You will be alright." I give her a kiss on the forehead. I might not have wanted to fall in love again. But if it is with her, I am willing to give her my all, just like I know she will give me her all.

"Mas..." She reaches up and puts her hand on my face. I smile down and kiss the palm of her hand. "Ben... and Marley..." Her eyes close again. Whatever it is will have to wait till we get her to the hospital.

I run down the stairs and see Jake waiting by an ambulance. I run over to them and they take Elena. "I have her sir." The paramedic takes Elena from me.

"She opened her eyes for a few minutes." I tell her as she goes over her vitals. He turns and nods at me as they load her into the ambulance. "I am going with her." He doesn't fight me on it, just tells me to get in. "Jake, meet us at the hospital. Make sure Marley doesn't leave your house."

"I am right behind you. Just need to answer a few questions." Jake turns and heads back towards the police officers. I could see Gramps just nodding at me in approval. I didn't even consider that he might want to go with her. But him giving me the approval, means a lot to me right now. I couldn't leave her even if they did pry me off her. I need to be there when she wakes up.

"She's going to be fine. She will have to spend the night in the hospital for observation." The paramedic pats my shoulder.

I feel the relief wash over me. "Do you know how a bee got to her? I mean it's 10pm, shouldn't bees be asleep at this time?" She looks at me with a questioning look. Hell if I knew I would have told her. I had the same question.

"I have no idea, but I am sure to find out. I will make sure no bees will ever be able to get near her again." I brush my finger along her jaw as the paramedic watches me.

"I hope I find a guy that cares for me the way you care for her. Your girlfriend is lucky to have you." I smile, never taking my eyes off of Elena.

"I am the lucky one to have her. She saved me, when I didn't even know that I needed saving." I lean down and kiss the top of her head. I would spend the rest of my life making up for my stupidity, if she would let me. As soon as she's better, I am going to tell her about my plans and that I don't care about them anymore. That I would never take her ranch from her. I also want her as my new lawyer. I know she might not want to leave the ranch and that's fine. I would travel between here and Chicago. I will make this work even if I have to end up moving out here to Montana for her. I would do that with a smile on my face.

CHAPTER 13 – ELENA

I feel as if a train has hit me. Everything is sore. I try to open my eyes, but damn sleep is so much better. I try to move my hand, but feel a weight on it. What the hell? My eyes shot open only to see Mason holding my hand in both of his as he lay on my arm sleeping. Jake was in the corner sleeping with a towel covering him. That man needs to learn to use blankets. He is always covered in something weird. I remember just after graduation we found him sleeping in the barn with one of the dogs blankets covering him and it was one of the small dogs. It didn't even cover his ass, like he wanted it too.

"Mas..." I poke his cheek with my other hand. He stirs but doesn't wake up. I giggle as he places a kiss on the back of my hand in his sleep. I am still upset with what he did, but we can work through it and be friends. We have all been betrayed by someone that was supposed to love us. Someone that told us they would do anything for us.

I lay there and just admire the beauty of a man laying here holding my hand. He really has the perfect face. I know it's cheesy. But him in a pair of cowboy boots and a cowboy hat might just make me fall even deeper for him. I know after everything that has happened, I shouldn't get my hopes up. But just looking at him makes me want to try. I want to see where this could go. I might just be a naive girl, but there has to be a reason we feel attracted to each other and it's not just sexual tension. I have a need for him. One that makes my heart beat faster just thinking of him, the way he smiles, the way his voice just flows through the air as he speaks.

"It's rude to stare." I chuckle as he lifts his head. "It is good to see those blue eyes staring back at me. I thought I lost you there for a moment." He cups my cheek with his hand, I lean into his touch, savoring the warmth of his skin against mine.

"Thank you for saving me. For some reason my Epi-pen in my bathroom was gone."He squeezes my hand. "But then after what I found out last night, nothing surprises me anymore."

"Elena, we need to talk. But it can wait till you are home." I try to read him, but there is nothing. He doesn't even look scared about this talk.

"Yeah, I have to tell everyone what Ben told me. He obviously planned to kill me. He basically said that he was going to tell me what their plan is, because I won't be around to stop him." Mason leans down and kisses my head. He has never been this attentive before. It is as if he was afraid that I would disappear.

He looks down at our hands. "How did the bees get to you?" I furrow my brows. Bees? I couldn't remember.

"I... I'm not sure. I can't remember that part. I remember Ben putting something on me. Then he opened my window, but after that everything happened so fast. Last thing I remember is you calling my name, just before everything went black." I remember feeling the relief of hearing Mason's voice. He was there when I needed him the most. Things could have been so much different if he didn't come in at that moment.

"She was covered in pollen. It would have made the bees a tad bit aggressive, wanting to get to it and take it back to their queen." A young doctor walks in with a smile on her face. "How are you feeling? I am Dr. Remi."

"I feel sore and a bit uncomfortable. But other than that I am fine." She nods as she walks over to me. She goes over my vitals not once acknowledging the two men in my room. The one who was still snoring away in the corner and the other one that was basically glued to my hand.

"You will be sore for a few more days. You were stung by three bees and lucky to be alive. The swelling has gone down, but I would still like to keep you here for tonight." She looks over to where Jake was sleeping and smirks at me. "The guys can stay if they want to." She leans a bit closer to me and so does Mason. She scrunches up her nose and narrows her eyes at him. "Do you mind?"

"Yes... I actually do mind." She shakes her head and straightens herself. She clearly knows he won't give up.

"You have two fine men right here. They almost had a fist fight with the other doctor, because they didn't want to leave you. Romeo over here..." She points at Mason. "He told us that he needs to be here when you wake up. You need to know that he would never let you go and would always be there for you." She smirks, while Mason puffs out a breath. His cheeks turn a bright shade of red. "And superman over there..." She points to Jake with his tiny red towel. "He told us that you would never forgive us if he wasn't in the room. He has to be here to keep you safe." I laugh at the two of them.

"Thank you for letting them stay. I definitely needed them when I woke up. Romeo over here has been there for me when I needed him. And Superman over there, always treats me to a laugh. I mean where the hell did he get that towel?" Mason laughs and shakes his head.

"That is my golf clubs' towel. He took it out of the truck. His words and I quote 'There are never enough blankets. I will need this.'" Mason makes some air quotes. Makes sense that the towel is for something like golf clubs.

Dr. Remi finishes my check up. "When he wakes up, send him to come and get some painkillers. He will be stiff and sore from the way he is sleeping." She walked to the door. She stops just before opening the door and glances at Jake again. She opens the door and walks out without another word.

"I think the doc likes Jake." I move to the side and pat the open space next to me without saying a word. "I don't want to hurt you."

"You won't hurt me. You must be tired. Let's just sleep for a bit more please." He slowly gets in bed next to me. He puts his arm around my shoulder as I snuggle up to him. This is what I wanted us to do the night we were out in that field. I just hope this time it ends differently.

Mason kisses the top of my head and I let his heartbeat lull me to sleep. "I will be here when you wake up. I am never running away from you again." I smile just before I let sleep take over.

❣

I have been home for a few days. Jake and Mason never leave my side. I am getting a bit frustrated, but to their defense, they just want to make sure I am safe. Ben was still out there. Even though the police had Marley in custody. They weren't able to find Ben at all.

I walk into the kitchen to see John and Alex sitting at the table. Wonder if there is something going on there. "Good Morning you two!" They turn their heads and give me a sweet smile.

"Where's your shadow this morning?" Alex asks with a raised eyebrow. I chuckle just as my grumpy best friend walks in after me.

"I am here..." He walks past me straight to the coffee pot.

Mason walks in after him. He stops next to me and kisses my cheek. "Can I get you some coffee?" I nod and he takes the pot out of Jake's hand.

"I had that first." He protested while trying to take the coffee pot back. Mason holds it out of reach.

"Down boy.... I am getting Elena a cup then you can down the rest." Jake huffs and folds his arms across his chest mumbling something none of us are able to understand.

I take a seat next to John and rest my head on his shoulder. "This is what mornings are made for."

"Have you and Mason talked yet?" I lift my head and look at John. I know we need to talk, but this feels so good. Having him here with me. Him holding me at night to make sure I am comfortable. But John is right, we need to talk.

"We will. Right after the detective leaves today." My eyes immediately find Mason's as I say that. His smile lights up the room and the sparkle in his eyes outshines the stars. These last few days since the hospital basically have been the best days of my life. I never felt like this with Ben. I never had the connection with him that I have with Mason. And I have only known Mason for two whole weeks now. But he makes me want more.

John puts his arm around my shoulder and leans closer to my ear. "He's a good one. Don't let him get away." I turn to look at him confused. "You don't know, do you?"

"Know what?" John checks if Mason is paying attention only to see that Mason was having a conversation with Gramps and Jake.

He takes a deep breath and leans even closer to make sure that only I hear him. "Mason phoned the night that Ben was here. They made it as if you were busy, then told him to send them his locations. Which he didn't. He said that he knew something was wrong. He used his GPS to get to the main gate. Then phoned 911 and told them you were in danger. He kept the operator on the line and ran all the way from the gate to the house. And well the rest you know." I wasn't able to say anything. Mason did all that for me. I look up only to see him staring at me again. He winks at me before he turns back to his conversation.

We are all interrupted by a knock on the door. "That should be the detective." Gramps says as he walks to open the door. Mason comes over to me. He rests his hand on my shoulder as he leans down to my ear. His hot breath sent shivers all over my body. The same tingle that I felt the first time I met him returns.

"Are you ready for this?" I turn my head slightly. His lips were so close to mine, I could just kiss him.

"Yes... I want this over with." He leans closer brushing his lips over mine before we could lock lips, Alex pulls Mason away. "Hey..."

"No lip locking, the detective is here." I turn to see Gramps and a well dressed man standing in the door. Gramps had this smile on his face that creeps me out. He knows something I don't.

We went to the living room. I need them to know what happened and what Ben had planned. Jake's mom and sister have also joined us.

"I'm Detective McNally. Now I believe that you know what their motive is. We have been trying to find information on Ben and Marley. But there is none." Jake and Mason share a look. I know this is going to hurt them more than it did me.

"I do... And I don't think that Ben and Marley are their real names anyway." Detective McNally nods. Mason takes a seat next to me and Jake goes to sit next to his mom.

Detective McNally takes out his notebook. Ready to take the information down. "Whenever you're ready."

I take a deep breath. I know that somehow we will have to find a way to make sure no one could ever try and rip up our ranches. I start by telling them how Marley and Ben had their eyes on Jake from the start, but they knew that he would never give Marley the time of day. They knew that Mason is a hopeless romantic and would give anything for the one he loved. They had Marley make him fall for him, doing everything that she knew would catch his attention. But she also seduced Jake and when she knew that Jake was ready to have her, she broke it off with Mason. I then tell them how Ben had his eyes on me after finding out that Ashford Hotels have been following my studies and were interested in having me as their lawyer. How Ben then got me to trust him only to make sure that I would leave and he could take over the account.

"Wait... How did he know about you? I didn't even know. My father said he had a lawyer in mind, she just needs to graduate first." Mason runs his hand through his hair.

"I have no idea. That is what he said." Mason puts his arm around my shoulders before giving me a kiss on the temple.

"You can carry on now." Detective McNally states. I give him a nod, taking Mason's hand in mine.

I explain to them about what Marley and Ben found out about the ranch. About the gold reef that runs through our ranches. I see Jake's face pales. I told them about the wedding and how they would have had them all killed in a plane accident, even mason.

Mason's arm around my shoulders tightens. His breath was uneven as I turned to look at him. "Mas... Breath...." I put my hand on his cheek and made him look at me.

"I have to ask. Is that why Ben tried to kill you?" I nod and look down. I have never been as scared as I was that night. I was sure I would never see anyone even again.

"Yes, he said he had a plan. I would die in an accident. Obviously the bees. He will inherit the ranch after I am gone."

Detective McNally goes through some notes, before he looks up again. "Did you ever have a will that states him as your sole beneficiary?"

"No, I never saw a future with him. I would have never left everything to him." Jake hangs his head and his mom pats him on his back. My eyes grew wide when I remembered my last will. "Jake, you get the ranch... Shit."

"Yes and Marley knew it. They were going to murder you then when I get the ranch they would have murdered us too. How could I have fallen for that. I should have seen through her." Jake states without ever looking up at any of us. I have never seen him like this.

Mason lets out a breath. "Jake, this is not your fault. They had this perfectly planned. Not one of us saw this coming." Jake finally looks up and gives Mason a nod. These people have no idea what their plan has done to good people. Jake will never trust anyone again. He has always been a bit closed off and now it will be worse.

"Is there anything else?" I think for a moment.

"Yes, Ben said that he and Marley were married. I don't know if that might help." Mason jumps up and paces the floor. He was having this internal battle.

"That bitch. They are married and yet they still sleep with everyone." He turns to me.

"Ben did say he knew she was doing you and Jake. She also knew that he was sleeping with me. Apparently I was just a good lay for him." Mason kneels down in front of me. He cups my face in his hands.

"Never believe what he says. You aren't just a good lay. You are so much more. You are the light that brings us together. You are the river giving us water. You are my lighthouse. I am so sorry it took me this long to see. That night you drove off, it felt as if my heart was ripped apart. I saw my future drive off. When I walked into that bathroom and saw you on the floor, just laying there. I thought that I had lost you. I was ready to give up, because I wouldn't be able to live without you." I feel the tears sting my eyes. We weren't supposed to do this in front of everyone. But I guess Mason couldn't wait any longer. "I never want to find out what life is without you in it. You make everything better. Ben never deserved you. Ben never knew what a diamond he had. You are the most beautiful woman I have ever seen. My raven haired, blue-eyed cowgirl." He leans forward, capturing my lips with his. It is not a forced or rough kiss, it is sweet and soft. Like he wants me to feel the words he just spoke.

"Mason..." Before I could say more everyone started clapping hands. We look at them and they are all beaming.

Gramps puts his hand on Mason's shoulder. "Now we can talk. You know her." I look between Gramps and Mason.

"What do you mean?" Mason just kisses me again before he stands up. He holds out his hand to me. I take it and he helps me up.

"Are we done here?" Detective McNally looks down at his notes before he turns towards me.

"We are. I will however need you three to answer some questions. But we can do that later. Let me see if I can find out who Marley and Ben really are." He shakes our hands and Gramps leads him out.

Mason turns to me. "Let's get out of here. I need to talk to you in private." I nod. Because let's face it. That was all that I could do. This man had me all mushy inside. "Guys, we will see you later."

"Don't go making any little Mason's..." Mason punches Jake in the arm, while Jake just laughs. He pulls me after him as he runs out the back door. He just keeps running and I try to keep up.

I pull his arm and he stops. "Mason... I can't run anymore." He pulls me closer to him. His lips connect with mine, his tongue teases my lips and I open for him. Our tongues dance together. He has his one arm around my waist while his other is tangled in my hair. My one hand is on his heart and the other plays with the hair at the nape of his neck. He slowly pulls away after a few minutes of our make out session.

"I just couldn't wait any longer." He leads me to a tree. He sits down and pulls me to sit down between his legs. "Elena, I need to tell you everything."

"I am ready to listen." I turn my body a bit to be able to see his face. He wraps his arms around me.

"When I was driving towards The Forester Ranch. I saw this ranch. It was the most beautiful place I have ever seen. I saw this as a getaway from all my stress and worries back home. Just seeing the lush green grass, beautiful stream and the mountains around it made me fall in love with it. I wanted to buy it, I knew it was a long shot, but I still wanted it." I bite my lip waiting to hear what he wanted to do with it. "I wasn't going to tear it up. I wanted to transform it into a hotel and spa. I wanted others to be able to experience it. Others are able to come here and relax, forgetting about their worries back at home. But I still wanted to keep the ranch feeling. I still wanted the owners of the ranch to take care of it." I could see that working here. People would be able to enjoy the outdoors and still relax. "I didn't know you were the owner. It never occurred to me. I did send Ben here, but he wasn't supposed to do anything else. He phoned me and told me the owner didn't want to sell. When I got here I found out that you worked here. Gramps never told me that he wasn't the owner. He told me to get to know you. To really get to know you. Then we can talk. I guess what he meant was that he didn't have a say in the ranch at all.

"No, he doesn't. But it sounds like something Gramps would do. He always wants to protect me. Do you still want to buy the ranch though." He looks at me surprised, before the most beautiful smile appears on his handsome face.

"No... This is your place." I give him a peck on the lips. "Anyway, all the time I spent with you made me fall for you. I tried to fight it, but I couldn't. You kept crawling into my heart. You kept chipping away at the wall I tried to build up. I couldn't fight it anymore. I thought I was too late when I saw you with John, but then found out he's gay. Then Ben had to open his big mouth. I was going to tell you everything anyway." He runs his hand up and down my back the whole time he talks to me. I could feel myself melting at his touch.

"Mas... I forgive you. I think we both just found out how short life could be. I don't want to waste time thinking about the what ifs. We can just move forward."

"I would like that. I want to see where this could go. I want to spend my time with you. I want you to be mine and only mine." I giggle at his sweet words. I want this more than anything.

"I want that too. But how would it work? I live here and you live in Chicago?" He runs his hand over my cheek before he plants a sweet kiss to my lips.

"Well, there is one more thing I need to talk to you about." He shifts a bit, still keeping me between his legs. "I want you to be my lawyer again. You should have been from the start. Now I know what you are thinking... You can still stay here. I will fly between Chicago

and here. And you can always come visit me."
He rubs the back of his neck nervously.

I look out over the land. The mountain
that is painted in red, orange and light pink as
the sun shines on it. This is my home, but
Mason also feels like my home. "El..." He says
with uncertainty.

"I would love that. Let's see how things
go. I want to see what we can be. If all works
out, we can move to one place." He pulls me
closer to him and I lay my head on his chest. I
heard the beat of his heart. It was as if it was
beating just for me, just like mine is beating
for him.

The future is uncertain for both of us. All
I know right now is that Mason makes me feel
things I have never felt before. He feels like
home. He feels like he is my missing piece. We
have so many obstacles ahead, but together
we will be able to handle all of them.

CHAPTER 14 - MASON

It has been four amazing months. Elena and I have been together for four months and we are only getting closer to each other even though we love miles apart. I have spent most of my free time in Montana with Elena. And on the times I couldn't go to her, she would come to me. I don't think my plane has ever flown this much. But I don't care at all. It's worth it to see the love of my life. I haven't said those three words yet. I am, however, telling her tonight. We have a charity function to go to. I can't wait to show off my beautiful country girl. She will always be my country girl. The only girl that has ever held my heart this tight. What I felt for Marley, I now definitely know wasn't love. I know what true love feels like now.

The police were able to track down Ben and convict him of attempted murder, unfortunately they had nothing on Marley and had to let her go. None of us have seen her in

the last four months. We all hope that she doesn't try to come back.

Alex has finally trusted us enough to tell us he is gay. He is now dating John. And even if I have to say it myself. They make a beautiful couple. Not as beautiful as me and Elena though.

Jake was still drake. Even after what Marley did to him. He didn't let it affect him at all. I admire him. I wish I was as strong as him. He told me that we all have a diamond waiting for us, we just have to go through glass first to get our diamonds. Who knew that Jake could be that romantic. The girl that gets him one day will be one lucky lady.

"Are you ready Mr. Ashford?" I lift my head from the documents in front of me only to see Jake standing in my doorway.

I smile at him as I get up and grab my jacket from the back of my chair. "I am. I can't believe how excited I am to see her. I saw her last week, but being away from her is getting harder for me. I want her with me all the time." I put my arms through the sleeves of my jacket, checking the time to make sure I am not late to pick her up from the airport.

"You should tell her!" I wipe around at the sweet voice I have missed most in the world. My heart explodes when I see my gorgeous girlfriend standing in my doorway next to my best friend.

"Sweetheart..." She runs over to me and jumps into my arms. I spin her around as our lips meet. I have missed this so much. I have missed her so much. "Damn, I missed you." She smiles as she rests her forehead against mine.

"You have no idea how much I missed you. Mornings on the ranch just aren't the same without you." I slowly put her feet back on the ground, still holding her against me.

"I am so happy you are here. How's Gramps?" She snuggles into my chest and I feel complete with her where she belongs, right here in her arms.

"He's doing good." She leans up and places a peck on my lips. "Now, are we ready for this charity event?" She raises her brow. I run my eyes over her body. She's dressed in a pair of jeans and a loose hanging shirt. Her favorite pair of cowboy boots completes her look. My one and only country girl.

"I am ready. Can I just say that you look perfect? You are the most beautiful girl in the world." I take her hand and lead her out of my office. The charity event is for the kids. We decided to do a fun fair. With games, food and rides.

We make our way over to the fairgrounds. Jake, Alex and John joined us. I walk with Elena through the sea of guests, holding on to her hand tightly.

"I need to have a word with my father." I point to where he is talking to some partners, one of which is Zena's father.

"Let's go. I am not leaving your side tonight. I have missed you way too much." We walk over to where my father is. She smiles as he sees us walking up to him.

"Mason, It's good to see you. And this must be Elena. She's even more beautiful than what you said." My dad kisses Elena's cheek.

"It's nice to meet you Mr. Ashford." She smiles sweetly as she snuggles into my side. I feel the pride watching her and my dad talking. He has never liked any of the girls I had.

"Elena! Let's grab some food." John pulls her away from me. "She will be back shortly." She laughs as she blows me a kiss.

I turn back towards my dad and I can see the worry in his eyes. "What's wrong dad?" He just shakes his head.

"Let's talk about it after the weekend. Spend some time with your girl. Things might change next week." With that he leaves me standing there alone. What does he mean? Things might change. There is nothing that can change. He has no say in Ashford hotels and casinos. I decided to move it to the back of my mind. I will not let it get me down. It will not ruin my weekend with my girl.

The rest of the evening we spend our time between rides and games. I won Elena a huge teddy bear which she gifted to a little girl and I swear my heart melted at the sight of that little girl with a bear twice her size.

"I want to show you something." She nods. I pull her with me to the far side of the fair. We stand by the pier looking out over the lake. I look down and see the girl I want to spend the rest of my life with. She's my everything.

"This is amazing." She snuggles into me. Just having her in my arms makes all my worries disappear. I love her with my whole heart.

"Elena... I love you." She looks up at me with tears dancing in her eyes. I just hope that it's happy tears.

"Mason... You have no idea how much I love you. Every minute with you is better than the one before." I smash my lips onto hers just as the fireworks goes off.

Was it magical... Yes. Just as magical as the girl in my arms. I want to spend the rest of my life making her happy. Showing her just how much I love her. I want to see our kids running around the ranch. Being as amazing as their mother. Maybe I am getting ahead of myself. We will see what the future holds for us. But for now, Elena Tate is the woman I am going to spend my life with and nothing will change that.

TO BE CONTINUED.....

A COUNTRY WEDDING

Mason has the girl of his dreams, but a deal his father made might ruin everything for him. He is pushed into an arranged marriage. Can he and his country girl find a way out of the wedding before it's too late. Will Mason have to marry the unwanted woman or will she help Mason reunite with his love.

Elena has everything, until the man she loves is taken from her. She spends day and night trying to find a way out of this arrangement. But when she receives shocking news. How will Mason react? And can it save them or is it too late?

This is the second book in the Country Series. Mason and Elena's love story continues.

SPECIAL THANKS

I would like to thank the following people that have been there for me.

My husband and kids - Thank you for helping me and supporting me.

To my two beautiful Beta readers - Colleen Darley and Jessica Bruno-Matlak. You ladies are the best. Thank you for all the chats, the laughs, even when I felt like pulling my hair out. Love you ladies.

My Bestie - Elsebe Luyt - Thanks for being my right hand, for always having my back. And listening to all my crazy ideas. Love you.

To my Arc reader - you guys are amazing.
Thank you for taking the time to read this for
me. Without you there wouldn't be a book.

My fellow author - Melony Ann - Thank you for
your insight and help. Thank you for all the
support. Love you.

To my Instagram bestie Aura_bud thank you
for this beautiful cover. For all the time we
spend creating it. Also for all the chats. Love
you girl.

To everyone else that has always been there
for me. Thank you all. This wouldn't have been
possible without each and everyone of you.

Love you all

Printed in Great Britain
by Amazon